# MILLIONAIRE GHETTO MOMS

# MILLIONAIRE
# GHETTO
# MOMS

Hustlin' is Not Just a Man's Game

A NOVEL

*Ukela A. Moore*

*&*

*George Darden*

iUniverse, Inc.
Bloomington

**Millionaire Ghetto Moms**
**Hustlin' is Not Just a Man's Game**

This is a work of fiction. All of the characters, names, incidents, organizations, and dialogue in this novel are either the products of the author's imagination or are used fictitiously.

iUniverse books may be ordered through booksellers or by contacting:

iUniverse
1663 Liberty Drive
Bloomington, IN 47403
www.iuniverse.com
1-800-Authors (1-800-288-4677)

ISBN: 978-1-4759-7010-4 (sc)
ISBN: 978-1-4759-7009-8 (ebk)

Printed in the United States of America

iUniverse rev. date: 04/11/2013

To all of the women out there who hustle to earn a living for themselves and everyone they love.

~ Ukela A. Moore

Dedicated to my fire on the inside;
Sherri, Sydney and Kayla.

~ George Darden

# ACKNOWLEDGEMENTS

To God; with Him anything is possible.

To My Mom, Albrice;
My first pencil, my first library visit,
My first piece of paper and much, much more,
I say thank you.

To My Children, Jade, Kenneth, Shawn & KeShawn;
It is an honor to witness your amazing spirits
and gifts, your futures are bright!

To My Brother, Charles;
My mirror in so many ways,
thank you for everything.

To A Fabulous Editor & Friend, Iyesha;
Thank you.

To My Husband, Terry;
My very own Mr. Incredible.

# INTRODUCTION

New Year's 2005

## Kimberly

"Malik!" Kimberly screamed. Her eyes widened in horror as she clutched the leather passenger side door with her right hand. She placed her left in front of her face, bracing herself for the unavoidable head-on collision with the oncoming vehicle. As she turned toward him, she could see Malik's jaw line clenched, his veins visibly rising in his hands as he gripped the steering wheel. As if everything was happening in slow motion, a thousand thoughts raced through Kimberly's mind; *Is this it? Is my life over? Will I see my children again?* She saw flashes of their children, Tre', Travis and Traniece. The twenty-five year old pair left them with their grandparents while they celebrated New Year's on the town this year.

Fourth Avenue was a two lane, one-way street in the middle of downtown, yet Malik and Kimberly were blinded by bright headlights coming from the opposite direction toward them. A crowd of New Year partyers on the way to their vehicles had begun screaming and running from the sidewalks toward the nearest building entrances when they saw the impending collision. When the two vehicles collided, the sound of the impact was deafening. The glass exploded as the compact, silver 4 door sedan that carried them, flipped over and over again on Fourth Avenue for what seemed like an eternity. Kimberly and Malik's bodies modeled rag dolls as the force of the vehicle tossed them violently about. In seconds, the sedan came to rest on its injured side. Kimberly opened her eyes to a thick wall of smoke but barely heard anything over the ringing in her ears and the blaring of a car horn.

"Malik." Kimberly said in a raspy voice that led into a coughing fit. Blood trickled down her forehead over her foundation. She kept looking toward what appeared to be the driver's side . . . calling for Malik. But she could not see him and she could not hear him.

"Lady, are you ok?" A strange man walked over and asked trying to focus on her face but still eyeing the mangled wreckage before him. The cars were still smoking, and he was visibly shaking from the nervous adrenaline at the gruesome scene that he just witnessed.

"Oh God, I saw everything!" Kimberly heard a bystander yelling nearby. She remembered the shrieking brakes and shattering glass moments before; the smell of brake fluid and burning rubber mixed with the cold air. She remembered that Malik had tried to miss the errant vehicle but it clipped them, sending them airborne and flipping out of control.

"Malik!" She strained to say.

"Miss, you've been in an accident," the man said regaining her attention, "don't try to speak, we've called an ambulance and they'll be here soon." Kimberly looked up at the man who was on his knees, looking at her, whispering to her so gently and reassuringly. "My husband . . ." Kimberly said drowsily, hearing the shrill of police sirens. "Where is Ma—. . . ?" Before she could finish her words, she had passed out.

# CHAPTER ONE

*People are always blaming their circumstances for what they are. I don't believe in circumstances. The people who get on in the world are the people who get up and look for the circumstances they want, and if they can't find them, make them.*

~ George Bernard Shaw

## Kimberly

## The Hospital

Kimberly could barely open her swollen eyes at Priest Lake Hospital to see her family members gathered around her. A blurred body moved toward her. As it did, she slowly recognized that it was her brother, DeMarco.

"Shhh . . . don't try to talk Kimberly." DeMarco said looking tenderly into Kimberly's eyes and holding her hand in his as only a big brother could. There was snow falling outside the window and she was covered with a crisp white sheet up to her chest.

"Am I in the hospital?" she whispered.

"Yes you are baby sis, and your family is here with you." Gathered in her room were Malik's mother, sister, brother, father, Kimberly's mother and stepfather and Malik's best friends Darius and Rodney.

Visibly holding back his own tears, he said, "I have something to tell you Kim." He paused and said, "Malik—" DeMarco was interrupted by a room full of whimpers that turned to torturous cries at the sound of Malik's name. With his eyebrows fixed into a sorrowful frown he finally uttered, "The accident that you and Malik were in was bad Kimberly—real bad. Ummmm . . . . Malik was brought here to the hospital with you, but . . ." DeMarco's voice began to crack at the sight of his sister's beautiful brown eyes welling with tears, "he passed away, Kimberly. I'm so sorry, I'm so sorry."

"Oh Go—" Kimberly shouted to the top of her lungs . . . Kimberly's mother rushed over to try to console her, but she was having none of it. She screamed, "No, no, no, no!" to the top of her lungs over and over again with the entire room chiming in with cries of grief. Malik's father marched out of the room, unable to deal with the sorrow that soaked the room. Three nurses rushed into the room to try to bring things back to a state of calmness.

"It's alright, Baby," Kimberly's mother, Genesa, grieved in unison with the heavy cries of the new widow Kimberly Mayes.

A couple of hours later, Kimberly drowsily woke from her sleep and almost instantly began crying again after looking around and remembering. "Where are my kids? Where are Traniece, Travis, and Tre," she said between whimpers.

"They're fine baby," said Malik's mother, Mrs. Mayes. Both Genesa, and Mrs. Mayes, who had gone to sit down across the room, shot back over to console her.

"They're with your aunt Lula." Genesa said referring to her sister.

Kimberly stared at the ceiling after hearing of their whereabouts and rolled over on her side in the hospital bed away from everyone. She lay with both hands tucked under the left side of her face pressed together as if in prayer. It was still snowing. It was New Year's Day 2005. "He's gone," she whispered forcing herself to think the thought.

*   *   *

## The Funeral

The sunrays bounced off the snow and made the day extra bright that early afternoon. Bright white light was transformed to color as it filtered through the stain glassed windows of the church on the country hill. The wooden cushionless benches reminded Kimberly of the days that she came there with her grandmother, who shared the same church home with Malik's grandparents. Church fans with the faces of little black girls praying lined the back pockets of the benches. Dark red song books shared the space and were scattered throughout the church. Kimberly's stomach was riddled with knots as the hour she dreaded approached.

Malik lay in front of her, in his casket, white suit contrasting with flawless dark skin. There was a small gash above his left eye that was carefully covered by makeup. His hair was cut low, wavy and his goatee was lined, still freshly trimmed from his trip to the barbershop the day before the accident. DeMarco squeezed her hand as she stared into his face. Her son Tre' was on the other side and beside Tre' were Mr. and Mrs. Mayes. Kimberly's mother, Genesa sat with Kimberly's stepfather on the other side of DeMarco, each holding one of the twins, Travis and Traniece. Kimberly leaned against DeMarco's shoulder and continued staring at the face that just a few short years ago; she looked into while saying, "I do". It was the same face she looked into while the doctors yelled, "push, Kimberly, push!" at the hospital on two occasions. The face she saw every night before she fell asleep and every morning when she woke.

A stout woman from the choir stepped down to the microphone and began to hum *Precious Lord, Take My Hand*. Mrs. Mayes had begun to rock from side to side and shake her head aggressively as if in disbelief. Mr. Mayes, tried to hold her, but she cut loose from him, ran over to Malik's casket and yelled, "Why, God, why? Why did you take my Baby, why? Oh Lord, Jesus, why?" Two ushers rushed from the back doors of the church, where they had been posted, to comfort the grief-stricken mother with a fan and gentle strokes on her back. The women in white dresses and white gloves made sure she did not fall and hurt herself while she stomped and yelled more forcefully. Her black loafers hoofed like thunder in the small church. As if the emotions were contagious, Kimberly's weep turned to an audible cry and DeMarco held her closer to him. Malik's mother, now overtaken with grief, began to fall out in front of the casket. She fell into the floor screaming and kicking and the ushers carried her from the church.

## At Home

At her apartment, Kimberly had been in bed for almost a week. Everyone in her family had been going in and out of her house since the funeral, especially Genesa and Mrs. Mayes. They left food, took care of the children, and took phone calls. Kimberly was oblivious to everything going on around her. The entire week was a blur and she had begun every single morning with a cry that lasted until she was exhausted and red-eyed.

Kimberly walked barefoot to the back of the plush carpeted apartment to Tre', room to see if he was still asleep. He was. She sat down in the rocking chair across from his bed. Malik wanted Tre' to be named after he and his father, making him Malik III. Everyone caught on to calling him Tre'. He represented the third Malik in the family. At 5 years old he was the spitting image of his father, dark skin, huge brown eyes, dimples and curly black hair.

"I remember when Tre' would sleep on Malik's chest when he was a baby." Kimberly said looking toward the entrance of the door as Mama Mayes walked into Tre's Little Bill themed room.

"I can't live here anymore . . . without Malik. There are too many memories. I can't—I can't bear to be here without him. And I don't care where I go I just need to get away from here."

Mrs. Mayes tucked her lips in and tears welled in her eyes. "I understand." she said. She walked over to Kimberly and kissed the top of her head then turned and walked out of the room. After sitting there for a few moments longer, Kimberly walked across the hall to the bedroom, immediately to the right of her cornered master bedroom. She looked down on Travis, who was also sleeping and over at Traniece who was wide awake and grinning with her feet doubled over and pulled happily into her mouth. Kimberly smiled and lifted her six month old baby out of her crib.

Travis and Traniece were a surprise duo. Malik and Kimberly knew that multiples were hereditary on Malik's side of the family, but they were still surprised that the gene landed upon them. Travis was a mixture of Malik and Kimberly, but Traniece looked more like her mother.

Kimberly had successfully rocked Traniece to sleep, then tip-toed into the living room where she and Malik had bought and placed their new Macintosh computer and searched the local listings for homes that she thought she may be able to afford.

# CHAPTER TWO

*The world is wide, and I will not waste my life in friction when it could be turned into momentum.*

~ Frances Willard

## Janice

Six-year old Tariq lay in bed staring at the ceiling, listening to his parents argue. It was 3am and his father had come in and slammed the door just a few moments earlier, jarring him from his deep sleep.

"Baby, you spent all yo' check?" Janice asked Jaurice, attempting to be quiet.

"Yeah . . . and?" Jaurice said nonchalantly. Stumbling as he grasped the forty ounce malt liquor bottle in his unsteady hands. He walked over to Janice. "Whatchu gon' do about it?" He laughed. "Imma grown man up in here!" He shouted, towering nine inches above Janice.

Twenty-eight year old Janice loved her husband Jaurice, but she was nearing the end of her rope from years of his abuse and antics. They had been together since high school, and had two children, six-year old Tariq and four-year old Porcha together. Unfortunately, the only thing that the honey complexioned woman seemed to have to show for it was the children, and a gash in her brow that made it difficult for her cousin Nessa to arch. It was constant reminder of the fight that they had back in 1999, the way they brought the new millennium in and every other weekend it seemed.

"The rent is due, the fridge is empty, but you can get a haircut first?" She said to him matter-of-factly speaking. She eyed the Kool-Aid colored stained carpet and shook her head. She would have to carry the burden of paying all the household bills alone . . . . again this month with her $5.15 per hour job. "What kinda man is that?" she said softly—almost inaudible. Almost.

"What did you just say?" Jaurice yelled an expletive and bloodied Janice's nose, then began tussling with her.

Tariq heard a loud boom, tussling, and his mother's scream. That is all that it took to send him and his little sister, Porcha, running toward their parent's bedroom.

"Stop fightin', stop fightin'!" Porcha cried.

"Git awffuh Mama, Deddy! Git awffuh Mama!" Tariq yelled, jumping up and down in his two sizes too small Spiderman pajamas. He cried as he watched his dad take his fist to his mother's face while she lay there helplessly pinned to the bed.

"AH" Janice cried out of breath from the struggle. "Sto—Jaurice, Stop!"

Jaurice ignored the two children. He immobilized her with the weight of his body. He had full control of her. Breathing heavily in the struggle, Jaurice began to choke Janice and exact another jab in her face, just as he'd witnessed his father do to his mother and girlfriends while growing up. "You don't disrespect me. I am a man! And you gon' learn that lesson today!" He said. She gasped for air and tried to get free of his grips. Finally, her left arm escaped and she managed to scrape the side of his face with her nails. He bolted up off of her, cursing, while running to the mirror.

"OOWWW!" Jaurice slurred another expletive after he looked into the mirror in disbelief at the sight of his bleeding jaw.

"It's (cough, cough) ok, kids . . . go back to (cough, cough) bed." She tried to say, hoarse and discombobulated.

Jaurice yelled profanities at Janice like rapid fire coming from an AK-47. He touched the stinging sensation of his wounds and looked down at the ground. "I'm sorry baby," he began in his drunken cry. Turning around he saw the flesh on the face of his children's mother swell and turn red and purple on her toffee skin. "Did I do that to you?—I messed up Baby, please, please forgive me, I messed up." He said in animation, shaking his head. He closed both his fists and rubbed his eyes with them like a sleepy baby that refused to take his nap. "Baby!" He shouted after her as she put her hand in the air and walked away.

Janice walked to the kitchen in a daze. She had nothing to say to Jaurice.

"Mama, you ok?" Porcha ran to her mother, took her hand and patted it while she looked at her father in fright and horror.

Tariq, only a foot away from Porcha stood still, unable to move, his fists clenched, lips pursed together, nose wrinkled and head tilted down. With crocodile tears in his eyes, his gaze was fixed on his father. He was breathing hard from adrenaline and saliva escaped his mouth with each breath.

The rest of the morning was sleepless and Janice Walker peered into the mirror of the one and only bathroom of the roach infested, rented two bedroom duplex. She wet the corner of a washcloth and wiped dried blood from the left side of her face, which had grown to be triple its' size.

She was able to get the children to bed after a lot of consoling. Jaurice lay on their bed on his stomach after his apology, and had been sleeping there like a baby since.

She sat down on the couch, putting her elbow on the arm of it, and rubbed her eyes with her hand. She had almost forgotten that she was on Capital Power's and Metro Water Department's shut off list until she heard the sound of a large truck followed by footsteps to the side of the poorly insulated duplex. It was the first week of the year and Janice did not think they would turn the service off. It was so cold outside. But within moments the television was interrupted by a blank screen, the lights disappeared in the kitchen and the lull of the refrigerator stopped. The paycheck Jaurice was supposed to bring home could have saved them from this.

Janice let out an audible sigh, as she tried desperately to think of who she had not worn out her welcome with, to borrow the money she needed to have the lights turned back on.

"With Jaurice's check gone," she explained to the church's pastor, "and my check used up for the rent, we're broke. I even washed some of the kid's clothes in the bathtub and hung them over the shower curtain rod so they would have something clean to wear to school, pastor."

"I understand, Janice. We love you child and we always will. We will help you out again this one last time, but you and your husband have got to work on your finances. I don't know what is going on in your house, but you are always the one asking and you know what the bible says about a man that will not take care of his family."

"Thank you," Janice whispered.

"Well not so fast Sister Walker. Since this is the third time that we have helped in the last six months, we can only give a portion of the bill and you'll need to bring your budget in, then after that, I'm afraid there'll be no more help for twelve months."

Janice agreed, worked out the specifics of when she'd be down to the church, and hung up her prepaid cell phone with the pastor.

"Anyone else's life would probably be better than this," she mumbled.

Porcha and Tariq heard their mother pulling out pots and pans in the kitchen, got out of bed and came in to sit down for breakfast.

Janice walked over to them in a daze with a box of raisin bran before she poured the last of what ended up being about an eighth of a bowl of cereal in each of their bowls and walked to the fridge.

She stared blankly at the empty milk jug sitting in the refrigerator.

She reached under the cabinet and pulled out a gigantic white box labeled "Powdered Milk" written in blue lettering. It was sitting beside a silver can that simply said "Pork" in black lettering and she pulled it out as well.

Jaurice rolled out of bed and went into the bathroom. A few minutes later he came out and slipped behind Janice and began hugging her from behind, whispering in her ear.

"Whatchu fixin' me for breakfast?" He chided, kissing her behind her ear, and then softly running his lips down the nape of her neck.

Janice tensed up but did not respond. Her eyes filled with tears and she shook her head in silence before turning to him and said, "Baby, I don't understand why you do me like this?" She allowed a tear to fall.

"You want me to apologize? Huh?" Jaurice yelled in Janice's face. "Huh? I'm sorry, baby. Forgive me, baby. There! Is that good enough? Oh no, wait I didn't get on my knees." Jaurice dropped to his knees sarcastically and yelled to the top of his lungs, "I want the perfect Ms. Janice Walker to accept my apology. I'm not worthy to be married to such an angel who never does anything wrong, ever. Please forgive me. Good enough?" He paused and stood back up to his feet. "Nawl, I bet it's not good enough." He said lowering his voice slightly while dusting the knees of his jeans off. "I don't need somebody always on my back telling me how wrong I am. I want to have a little fun sometimes." He put his finger in Janice's face. "So I'll tell you what, you can do this on your own, I'm out." He threw his hands in the air and walked toward the door.

"Deddy don't go!" Porcha said rushing up behind him, grabbing at his ankles. "Get back, Porcha!" he commanded, shaking her off his leg.

A nervous Tariq had stood, his hands balled in a tight fist again watching his father.

Janice sat down on the floor in front of the oven, covered her swollen face with both hands and wept.

An hour later, a loud knock on the door rattled Janice out of her daze. She got out of bed and walked to her door. "Who is it?" She asked.

"You know who it is!" Janice's Aunt GG said.

"I'm busy right now, can you come back later?" Janice said through the door.

"Busy doin' what? You better let yo' deddy's baby sister up in there oughta' this cold!"

Janice reluctantly opened the door and turned her back to go into the kitchen.

"What happened up in here?" Said the dark-complexioned woman with a comb lodged in her short, dry afro after Janice let her in.

"Nothin' Aunt GG and please close the door tight." Janice said to her before she plopped down on the couch. Aunt GG lived two duplexes down the street, courtesy of the Section 8 program, as opposed to Janice and Jaurice who were not on the program and were paying the full $700 rent for the two bedrooms.

"Why yo' TV don't work?" Aunt GG said, tossing her coat on the side of the couch and pressing the remote's power button. "Awww . . . girl. Yo' lights off too?"

Janice set the plate full of dishes into the sink, ignoring her Aunt GG.

"I came over here 'cause I need to watch Days of Our Lives! Have you seen it lately?" Aunt GG started walking over to the sink where Janice was. "I needs to watch tuh-day! Girl Marlena—what done happened to yo' face?" Aunt GG screamed, as she saw her for the first time.

Janice just looked at her Aunt GG.

"Keep on lettin' him beat on ya' if you won't to . . ." she said sarcastically.

Janice looked back down at the dishes in the sink. "You know Grandmamma didn't believe in no divorce and is that what you came over here for? To bother me? Huh?"

Yo' Grandmamma'—my Mama—ain't here getting her face pounded in! And that's real. You can keep holdin' onto that 'Old Time Religion' if you want to", Aunt GG said, "but God don't want you to go through hell on earth. I know that and I don't even go to church."

Aunt GG pulled out a cigarette and lit it.

"I know you saw my Deddy whip on my Mama when you was little, ok."

"And she loved him THROUGH his issues," Janice interjected.

"Issues? Don't a black eye and swollen face make that *yo'* issue? And that don't make it right. I told you she ain't here. You got to start thinkin' for yo' self baby girl—told you that a long time ago when you got with his triflin' behind, giving up school and your music. You could play the piano like nobody's business. People came to church just to hear you play and leave before the preacher got up to preach!" She laughed and took a whiff of the smoking stick. "And at least then you was goin' to church. Now you ain't even doin' that. What would yo' grandmamma say about that, huh? Since you doin' everything you thought she wanted you to do. Mama ain't happy with this, niece . . . she ain't happy at all." Aunt GG looked around at the mess resulting from the latest altercation. Then she turned to look at Janice. "You ain't got to believe me, but it's been plenty of women where you standing and some of 'em didn't make it through the next "issue". I gotta go." Aunt GG grabbed her coat, walked out and closed the door behind her.

Janice walked to the bathroom to look at her face again and thought of what her Aunt GG had said to her. Her eye was throbbing.

She went to the freezer to get some ice for her face. The ice was melting. She opened the refrigerator. Both spaces were empty, but it was getting as cold inside the apartment as it was inside there. She needed to go and get more food to get them through the next week. After standing in the kitchen with the ice on her eye for a few minutes, and eating a couple of spoonfuls of her morning helping of Argo starch, Janice put on a jogging suit and a coat and looked in on Tariq and Porcha napping. She ran out and found Aunt GG up the street in front of her duplex talking to a man who was leaning up against his car playing loud music.

"Can you run down and check on the kids while I go to the store?" Janice asked. "They're asleep." Janice had to literally yell over the music to her aunt, though she stood right beside her.

"Yeah, girl. Imma brang 'em up here though. I'm waitin' on a phone call." Aunt GG said.

She said between quick drags of the "cigarette." "Don't be gone long, neitha."

Janice jogged away. "You got some money?" Aunt GG asked, yelling after her. "Pick me up some mo' of that starch, then." She said before Janice had a chance to answer.

"I got some at the house." Janice yelled back to her aunt, jogging toward her neighbor's front door.

She knocked on the door and it was opened by Mr. Duke's great-granddaughter. The chatty teen flinched at the sight of Janice's face, but otherwise did not skip a beat on the phone as she opened the door for Janice and pointed toward the back of the house where the seventy-five year old man sat watching television.

"Oh, I didn't want to ask him anything," she said shaking her head, "I was wondering if you could run me to the store." Janice asked.

"Yeah." the young girl said unenthusiastically. She got off the phone and went to grab her grandfather's keys to his old Buick.

The girl's grandfather, Mr. Duke, had instructed his live-in granddaughter to always take Janice where she asked to go in his Buick. Living next door, he had found that her husband was notorious for taking their one and only car and leaving them without food or a way to get anywhere. Jaurice had gotten drunk last fall and had beaten Janice worse than ever before, then left. Afterward, Janice had knocked on Mr. Duke's door crying. He had winced when he saw her face. After inviting her in, he said, "You 'gon need some stitches for this one, sweetheart." He had heard them through the paper thin walls of the duplex often, yelling and tussling in the middle of the night. He didn't say anything negative to her, only that she needed a doctor and then proceeded to take her to the hospital.

Mr. Duke had heard the voices up front and knew that it was Janice. Slowly, he raised his tall, lanky, body from his bedroom chair, walked through the vintage room separator beads and peered around the corner into her face. She looked back at him briefly and dropped her head in shame. She knew he had heard the latest episode that morning through the thin walls of the duplex and now he had seen her face. Janice turned and walked to the passenger side of the car . . . feeling Mr. Duke's gaze still on her.

"Thanks, I got a ride back, but I might need a ride to Mount Ebenezer later on." Janice said as the granddaughter stopped at the market's entrance and let her out.

"Ah-ight." the girl said, anxious to get back home and pick up on her phone conversation where she left off. She pulled off as soon as Janice closed the door.

*Ok, this is the last time.* She whispered to herself and she walked through the grocery store's automatic doors.

Janice did not grab a basket. She walked to the magazine section, looked through a couple of magazines, then walked straight to the meat aisle. She grabbed some bologna and hot dogs and put them under her coat. Then she walked back up the same aisle that she just walked down ten minutes earlier and attempted to walk out of the front sliding doors . . . . two steps outside, she heard a man yell in a demanding tone "MISS, STOP MISS!"

*   *   *

Janice sat in her cell, eye swollen and black, purple and red, bruises on her arm and legs and missing her children. She stared helplessly at the cell wall. She'd been there for only two hours but it seemed like an eternity.

"You made bail, Mrs. Walker."

"Huh?" She said to the guard. "I didn't call nobody."

The bailiff walked Janice out of the cell and to the desk. Standing there was Mr. Duke. With his signature top hat, overcoat and cane, he silently signed the paperwork on the lines the policeman pointed out to him. Janice looked at him in disbelief, but he never looked up at her from constructing his signatures.

"You didn't have to do this, Mr. Duke." Janice said as they walked out together.

Mr. Duke didn't say a word, just adjusted his hat to make sure to shield his bald head from the cold.

Janice got back into the same car she had been in just three hours ago and left the police station.

"How did you know I was here?" Janice asked him, still in disbelief.

"My granddaughter," he finally spoke, "stopped at that little hair place next to the store and said she saw them taking you away in handcuffs. I know you got the two little ones at home. I ain't family or nothin' but you betta than this. I had a daughter and she was just like you" . . . . he paused. "You just betta than this," he finished softly.

Mr. Duke navigated the car carefully so he wouldn't hit any of the ice patches starting to form from the day's rain. He pulled up to their duplexes and Janice got out of the car in silence.

"Thank you, Mr. Duke." She said again solemnly and walked up the two steps to her empty duplex.

Janice walked into the bedroom amidst all the clutter, looked under her bed and pulled out a box. Inside was a bag of weed, the papers and clips that Jaurice kept there. She had taken a hit a couple of times in the past but never smoked consistently. Now, she needed the release. She took out two thin papers, licked the end of one of them and pasted them together. Dipping her hand into a zip lock bag, she gathered a moderate amount of the leaves of ganja and sprinkled them in the middle of the paper and carefully rolled it. Shamefully, she lit it and huffed slowly on the fresh joint. To ease her mind she clicked the battery operated clock radio on low. Tracie Spencer's *Tender Kisses* played and soon she felt a fierce buzz.

# CHAPTER THREE

*If you take responsibility for yourself, you will develop a hunger to accomplish your dreams.*

~ Les Brown

## Chrsyta

Chrysta Perry sat in the passenger seat of the shiny, new black Lexus. Raymond Meadows, a thirty-eight year old married professional and the latest suitor of Chrysta, had parked it along the curb in front of the apartment Chrysta shares with her grandmother. Slowly, he handed the twenty-one year old bi-racial beauty, a small box. Raymond looked around at his surroundings nervously. It was getting dark and the projects were beginning to come alive with cars, zooming by with their stereos blasting and young boys hanging out in the streets and on the corners.

Kanye's *Slow Jamz* played so softly in the background, only the bass line could be heard. "What's this?" Chrysta asked with a high-pitched voice.

"Open it." Raymond replied and smiled, looking around again at his environment.

Chrysta gently took off the lid of the box and her mouth opened wide. Inside was a bottle of imported Indian jasmine oil.

"Ooh!" She exclaimed and briskly sprayed some on her wrist.

"You like?" Raymond asked.

"I love." She answered softly.

Her smile faded into a look of concern, "When are you leaving her? I'm getting tired of only seeing you a couple times a week, Raymond."

Raymond sighed loudly.

"I know you don't want to hear this," she said, "but I feel like I need to remind you that you told me four months ago that it was over between you two, that your bags were basically packed. I want us to be together. Start off fresh. Ya' know."

"It is going to happen," he spouted, as gently as he could to hide the agitation. "Trust me. You won't have to wait too much longer. I just need a little time to square some things away. Then it's gonna be on." He smiled and tucked his large-boned hand under her chin and turned her pained expression filled face toward him. "Me and you, my little princess, forever."

Inside Chrysta's apartment, a light popped on. Chrysta sighed in disappointment while a flimsy, tin screened door opened.

"Who's 'dat? Who's there?" An old woman's voice yelps out.

Chrysta grinned at Raymond in acceptance and turned down the radio lower from the Jesse Powell song and pressed the window button lever to lower it halfway.

"Chry-stuh, is that you?" The old woman said.

"Yes. It's me Mama Jane." Chrysta replied, when she realized it was her grandmother calling.

Mama Jane was Chrysta's maternal grandmother and has had custody of Chrysta since she was born. She has always been highly protective and watchful of Chrysta, especially since Chrysta already had her own first child, four-year old Morgan.

"I'll call you tomorrow baby. It's getting late anyway. I don't wanna be out here any longer than I have to be." Raymond stated.

"Ah. So you tryin' to talk about my hood?" Chrysta asked. She was half joking and half serious.

"Gotta run. I'll call you, baby." Raymond said looking at Chrysta before allowing his eyes to dart around some more.

Chrysta placed her perfume in her purse and muddled into the house, disappointed at the intrusion of her privacy.

"Who was that in that big 'ole fancy car. Huh?" Mama Jane asked.

"He's just a friend of mine, Mama Jane. That's all."

"Well, I done told you to stay oughta' all these men folks face 'fore you get knocked up all over again. Ya' got one you can hardly take care of now . . . don't need annuddin," she said.

Chrysta walked into her room and lay on her bed and turned on her radio. Keyshia Cole's *Love* belted through the speakers as she thought of

Raymond. She smelled her wrist as she stared at a snapshot a friend had taken of the two of them about a month ago when he took her to the Elk's club.

She had come to know Raymond well during the past nine months. He was a pharmaceutical salesman for a major drug company and was, 'well-to-do', which is how her Mama Jane described all people like him. He met Chrysta at a gas station near the Elk's club after seeing her there earlier that night with friends. Looking at their picture, her thoughts migrated to Jonathan Baker, her daughter, Morgan's father. From an early age she had been shy, but keenly interested in boys. Chrysta's mother, Deidre, was a drug addict who fed her crack habit by turning tricks in the streets adjacent to General Oaks. Chrysta was the product of a random Jon who got her mother pregnant at the age of nineteen. The Jon, a dark-haired, married country boy roamed the streets from time to time in between his lunch hour on his construction site in search of a quickie. Always wanting to sample the other side of the racial divide, his co-workers often bragged about how many black whores were "up there" around the projects and he decided to get him one.

A few months into Deidre's pregnancy, the Jon had moved on to another site somewhere in the city, far removed from Deidre's tiny zone. Mama Jane had managed to have Deidre committed to the state hospital as soon as she got wind of Deidre's pregnancy. There she was forcefully detoxed and primed for Chrysta's birth after Deidre refused any abortion options. Then, Jane Marie Perry, Mama Jane as Chrysta called her, took custody of Chrysta after she was born and Deidre immediately hit the streets again and resumed her old lifestyle.

Two weeks later, Chrysta and Morgan were on the ten o'clock number 25 Midtown downtown to the vital records office. Chrysta knew she would need to get copies of their birth certificates to add to the info she would be keeping in the study of their new apartment. Raymond had shown her pictures of the new place and she was excited about finally having a place to call her own. It was the largest space that Chrysta had ever been in and was on the city's east side; a two-bedroom outfit with a nice spacious kitchen, living room, study, dining room and even a deck for outdoor entertaining. The complex had a pool, fitness center and clubhouse available to all the tenants. This is where Chrysta and Morgan would live until Raymond's "situation" had been resolved and then he would join them.

Besides Chrysta's excitement about this new life, she had not found the right time or right way to break the news to Mama Jane. She was in good health, but was getting older. Chrysta loved her grandmother but was ready to strike out on her own. General Oaks had become stagnant to her. The place she called home for twenty-one years was smothering her. She wanted more for her daughter and more for herself—more space and a place to be proud to come home to and entertain family and friends.

It was 4pm and the clouds gathered downtown as the sky turned gray.

"Looks like it's getting ready to rain." Chrysta said to Morgan, frowning and playfully poking her lip out. "I'd better call Raymond so we can pick up our stuff before it gets too late."

Chrysta went over to the office's public phone and dialed Raymond's number while humming a sesame street tune to Morgan. His voicemail picked up.

"Ray, it's C. I'm still downtown. Are you on your way over to get us? Call me back, ok? Love you!" Chrysta blew a kiss in the phone before hanging up. Chrysta kissed Morgan's cheeks and tickled her round belly underneath her Minnie Mouse coat until she shook with laughter.

Chrysta and Morgan went and sat outside on the huge steps of the government building and waited for Raymond. Twenty-five minutes had passed and Raymond was still not there. She frowned and placed her hand against her forehead as if in a salute to see if she could see him in the distance. She went back in to use the phone again but there was another woman there arguing on it with someone. It was the only working phone, so Chrysta waited until the woman got off and then redialed his number. His voicemail picked up again.

"Hey, Raymond, where you at? I'm not sure where you are, but we've been waiting for you a long time and I need you to come get us."

Moments later, it seemed like the sky burst open as a torrential rain began that would inevitably freeze later on that night. Upset, she huddled with Morgan into a corner under a canopy nearby, where others were gathered to avoid the rain. Their furniture was to arrive that evening at the new apartment, Raymond had told her. And surely he had gotten her voicemails.

Another hour passed and the cold rain had not let up. Chrysta was livid.

"I'm hungry Mommy." Morgan complained.

"I know baby." She replied. "We're getting ready to go."

They sat there and watched the last group of government workers dressed in sneakers and dress clothes filter out of the building and trot to the shuttle that took them to their parked cars.

Chrysta reached into her purse and searched for some extra money to ride the bus back home and found nothing. She checked her coat and jeans pocket but found nothing there either. Still raining, she could see the bus stop across the street was filled with people all trying to avoid the raindrops.

A dark blue Magnum pulled up and honked its horn. Chrysta glanced back but thought nothing of it. She heard it blow a second and third time as the window slid down letting the chorus of Snoop's *Drop It Like It's Hot* escape.

"Hey baby." A young man with cornrows said. "You and lil' miss need a ride?"

# CHAPTER FOUR

*Lots of people limit their possibilities by giving up easily. Never tell yourself this is too much for me. It's no use. I can't go on. If you do you're licked, and by your own thinking too. Keep believing and keep on keeping on.*

~ Norman Vincent Peale

After a long winter, the April streets of General Oaks were mostly lifeless except for the flowers the city planted along the edges of the sidewalks. It was part of the city's new beautification efforts, particularly in the projects. The apartments were two story brick; most dwellings were two bedroom outfits with both bedrooms upstairs and the kitchen and living room downstairs. Being in the south, they were somewhat smaller in scale, about nine hundred square feet total, compared to the dwellings in the larger northern cities, and ran more horizontal than vertical.

Residents did their best to keep a certain level of decorum on their porches; potted plants and oriental wind bells adorned some patios. But the norm was small barbeque grills, worn out sneakers and old children's bikes. One patio had a complete weight set along with a Nordic Track elliptical ride to compliment. The smell of freshly dumped trash in the communal dumpster permeated the April air with an odd combination of detergent, pinto beans and urine. Certainly not one of the city's worst housing projects, but a far cry from being a place that the mostly single mom occupants, wanted to live a long time.

## Chrysta:

Across the street in General Oaks, Chrysta's daughter Morgan, was glued to the window anxiously waiting to see her Mommy. Chrysta had been in and out so much lately, she hardly saw her daughter or her grandmother.

Chrysta pulled into her driveway in Mama Jane's 1986 Cutlass Supreme. She was getting more impatient than ever to move to a place of her own—especially since the plan with Raymond did not work out. She turned the key and as soon as the door opened, Morgan came running to her mother. Chrysta lovingly embraced her daughter.

## Kimberly

One block over from General Oaks, Kimberly walked around the tiny kitchen island in her newly renovated 1970's brick bungalow and pulled the banana bread out of the bread maker. Beside it was the small radio Malik used to keep in their master bathroom in the apartment she just moved out of. She turned the volume up when Mario's *Let Me Love You* came on. The air outside was still cool, but the house was warm and smelled of freshly baked bread. The twins were asleep and Tre' was playing in his room while she tended to her guest, her brother.

As soon as DeMarco heard that his sister Kimberly had moved, he planned a trip home to check on her and the kids.

"Nothing is too important for me to stay in New York when my baby sister needs help dealing with such a life altering change as what has happened to you . . . . not even medical school." DeMarco said.

DeMarco was almost ten years her senior, and was in med school in New York. He got off to a late start, but at thirty-two was realizing his dream of becoming a doctor. His caramel complexion was a couple shades lighter than Kimberly's; he was six feet two inches, single and did not have any children. He was engaged briefly, but after that didn't work out he decided to focus on his career.

"You would tell me if things were getting to be too much to handle, wouldn't you? I mean if you needed to take a trip somewhere and get away, you would tell me, right?" DeMarco asked, standing in Kimberly's new home with one hand in his jean pocket and the other muscular arm extended up, casually gripping the frame of the kitchen doorway.

"I don't need you to come to my rescue all the time Marco," she said refusing to let him take pity upon her. "I'm ok. I'm learning how to deal with the kids by myself and it is hard, but I don't have a choice so I'm doing it. I'll be fine. How is school?" She asked quickly, attempting to change the subject.

Choosing to be satisfied with her answer for now, he said, "It's good, real good. I'm glad it's almost over so I can come back home to my family . . . Have you decided to go back to school next year?" DeMarco asked walking over and gently leaning against the fridge closer to her.

"I need to take on a second job to clear some of these debts. We'll see though." Kimberly answered, not looking at him.

"Uncle Marco!" Tre' ran out of his room and into his uncle's waiting arms.

"What up knuckle head?" DeMarco said embracing his nephew while rubbing his head. "You need a haircut. Imma hook you up before I go, so you can look fresh, ah-ight?"

"Ah-ight." Tre' said. He beamed at the sight of his uncle.

"Oh, I think the twins are up," Kimberly said as she took off her apron and headed for the back bedrooms to grab them out of their cribs and bring them into the living room.


## Janice

Down the street in General Oaks, it was all work and no play for Janice on that sunny but cold Saturday afternoon.

Two and a half months ago, Tariq's teacher at school discreetly gave Janice a card to a hotline for abused women. Janice had secretly been speaking to a counselor via phone, and had been made to question her beliefs about what a relationship was supposed to look like and what she wanted out of a relationship. Her counselor had helped her to plan her exit from the abusive life she was used to. With an apology toward heaven to her grandmother, Janice snuck out of the house with the children and stayed in a shelter for a couple of days before she got a call back from General Oak's case worker that the apartment that she was on the list to receive was ready to move into.

She moved with only the clothes on her and the children's back and one duffle bag that she fit as much of their belongings in that she could.

However, the teacher had also referred her to a couple of other charities that helped women in her position get back on their feet and they were delivering a couch and some other items to her home today.

"Thank you so much." Janice said. She shook the hands of the gentlemen who brought all the furniture and lamps inside and set them up.

"If you need anything else, anything at all, give us a call." He said and handed her a business card. "We're concerned for you and your children."

"Thank you." Janice said.

They got into their rented moving truck and left.

Suddenly, while walking back up to her door, she felt nauseated. She had been that way off and on for a couple of weeks now. "I'm so sick and tired of all this drama," she said to herself, "that's probably it." She and Jaurice had continued their pattern 'til the end, going from fighting to making up, then fighting to making up, until in between she made her move.

When she and Porcha entered the house, she promptly let go of her breakfast on the kitchen floor. Like a light bulb, as she cleaned it up, it occurred to her that she needed to check her calendar for cycle dates. With everything that was going on, she had not been keeping up.

"OH, NO!" she thought, "I can't be."

# CHAPTER FIVE

*The greatest mistake you can make in life is to be continually fearing you will make one.*

~ Elbert Hubbard

50 and The Game's *Hate it or Love It* blasted through Chrysta's boyfriend's blue Magnum Friday night as he sped through the neighborhood to pick her up. Chrysta heard him coming from a mile away and grabbed her purse, kissed Morgan on the forehead, yelled to Mama Jane that she was gone for the evening and skipped out toward the car.

Cedric was Chrysta's latest lover. She had been dating him since the day Raymond left her and Morgan downtown in the cold pouring rain.

Ced, as he was known, was a self-proclaimed thug. His occupation, he said, was an urban clothing distributor for a "friend". At twenty-three, he wore braids, long shirts and baggy, beltless pants, which occupied one hand 100% of the time every time he had to walk somewhere. Chrysta found him to be both, enticing and dangerous. They did not have great conversation but there was something about him that was attractive and most importantly, he was present, and to Chrysta that was huge. In fact, he could be there for her, whenever she needed or wanted him to be. He adored her.

"Chrysta," Mama Jane yelled, "Come back here!"

Chrysta held one finger in the air toward Ced and mouthed the words, "I'll be right there."

"She stepped onto the porch where her grandmother stood and said, "Yes Ma'am?"

"Do you remember what I said about—"

"Yes, Ma'am I do," Chrysta interrupted. She leaned in and raised her brows, "Mama Jane, I'm not that stupid. I already learned that lesson and I have goals now." She smiled at Mama Jane and Mama Jane smiled back at her as she turned to walk away.

"That's alright with me as long as you remember that, chile. Oh, and Chrysta," Chrysta turned back around, "don't make no plans, I need you to be here all day long tomorrow afternoon, ya' hear?"

"Yes ma'am. What's going on?"

"The case worker at the office said that two girls that moved nearby a short while ago are needin' some help with watchin' their churren' while they worked or went to school. Since I haven't had anybody else other than Morgan, I went ahead and I told her to tell them to come over for Sunday dinner so we could meet 'em."

"Ok, I won't make any plans, Mama Jane." Chrysta said. She got in the car and they pulled away.

*   *   *

Kimberly cooked all morning between reading her African-American business based magazine and attending to the children.

"I have to start getting everyone ready so we can go and meet your new babysitter Tre', so I need you to help me with Travis and Traniece. I need you to go get their diaper bag and put 6 diapers in it. Ok?"

Tre nodded and did as he was told.

Kimberly looked around at her first home. She realized that she had not had time to enjoy the fact that she had purchased a home for herself and she didn't want to. She hadn't wanted it to happen this way—without Malik, or because of Malik. The survivor benefits from the government were taking care of her and the children, but last week she decided that it was time to get up and get her career back on track. Finding child care was the first step. She crossed her fingers and hoped for instant chemistry with the woman she was told that she would meet today, Ms. Perry.

*   *   *

Around the corner, Janice prepared for her sister Karen and her husband, Timothy to come visit that Sunday morning after their early church service and before she was due to meet her potential new babysitter, Ms. Perry.

Karen and Janice were total opposites but they loved one another and had grown close over the years. Sharing only the same father, Janice did not grow up in the same home and did not know she had a sister until she was a senior in high school. Since then she and Karen had always been there for each other, Karen treating her like the little sister she never had. Karen was one of the people Janice worried about wearing out her welcome with. Her lifestyle for the past 6 years had been draining. She was ashamed and it was a large part of her motivation for leaving.

Karen and Timothy pulled up in their black extended SUV. They were the epitome of the power couple. Timothy, several years older than Karen, was an architectural engineer. Karen was thirty-two, four years older than Janice, and was a tenured professor at a community college. They met in college and had one eight-year-old son named Timothy Jr., who everyone called T.J.

As Timothy walked around the SUV to open the door for Karen, Janice watched in admiration from the window, then gently opened the door and walked outside and greeted them. They were elated to see each other. Karen and Timothy had both expressed how proud they were of Janice, over the phone, to take her future into her own hands and start living life.

"Janice." The petite and older version of her said as she ran to her with a pained smile on her face. Karen embraced her little sister. "I'm proud of you." Karen had come over last year and saw Janice's face after a mild incident and it took everything within her to keep her and Timothy from confronting Jaurice.

Tariq and Porcha saw the truck out of the upstairs bedroom window and bolted down the stairs and yelled, "Uncle Tim! Aunt Karen!"

"What's going on man?" Timothy said to Tariq, giving him the usual hug and hand gesture that they normally exchanged. The only time that Tariq totally came out of his shell was when his Uncle Tim was around. T.J. hopped out of the truck and all the children began to talk and play. It was the most relaxed Janice had seen Tariq in a long time. Porcha took her aunt Karen by the hand and led her upstairs.

"Come see my new room Auntee Kay," she smiled and shouted. "Tariq don't stay in here, it's mine," she continued with a country drawl in her deep raspy voice.

"Well, I love it! I absolutely love your new room. Why don't we get these curtains out and start decorating it!" Karen said, winking at Janice as she joined them in the room.

As with all four-year olds, Porcha stayed and helped with the curtains that Karen brought for two minutes, then headed downstairs to go out and play.

"Thanks for coming, Karen," Janice whispered, coming into the room with her sister.

"It's no problem, Janice. We love you!" She said. "We haven't talked in a while, Janice. How are you? I mean are you sleeping? Are you eating?" Karen asked. "I may not have experienced a break up like this, but I've had my share of bad relationships in college before Timothy. I'm here for you."

"I know you are. I thank you. And I haven't been eating honestly. My stomach has been feeling kind of queasy, but it's cool. I'm sure it's just all this." Janice said. She waved her hands around indicating the move and the kids.

Janice and Karen talked for two more hours while they decorated and Timothy took T.J., Tariq and Porcha out to the park. Then they said their goodbyes and Janice got Tariq and Porcha ready for Sunday dinner at the neighbors.

At 2pm sharp, there was a knock on Mama Jane's door. She placed the large spoon that she was stirring the greens with, down in the middle of the stove, placed the top on and went to open the door.

"Hi baby, my name is Jane Ann Perry but people call me Mama Jane. Come on in." She said to Janice and gave her a warm hug she didn't expect. Janice hugged her back and introduced her to Tariq and Porcha.

"What a handsome boy and pretty little girl y'all are," Mama Jane said bending down toward them. "I bet these churren smart as a whip." She said smiling at Janice. "You can gwawn over and sit on the couch, baby."

As Janice led Tariq and Porcha to the couch and they all sat down, she heard The Canton Spirituals *Father I'm Coming Home* playing softly on the radio in the background and began to hum along under her breath. The smell of turnip greens and cornbread baking in the oven overrode the pumpkin spice plug-in that Janice saw next to the dark flower-patterned couch.

"I'll be witcha' in a minute baby, I'm just takin' the cornbread out the oven," Mama Jane yelled over her shoulder from the kitchen, only a few short steps away.

Kimberly packed Tre', Traniece and Travis into the 2002 Camry and drove it around the corner into General Oaks. She searched for apartment 103 and found it almost immediately. She parked on the side curb of the street behind a Cutlass. Each dressed in light jackets for the April wind; Kimberly pulled the twins out of the car and sat each on one of her hips. After getting one door closed, Tre' hopped out of the middle, closed the other door and kept pace with his mom to the apartment with the large baby bag. Travis tugged at Kimberly's freshly-permed hair pinned in a ponytail with laser-focused ambition while Traniece constantly looked around. She arrived at the door and knocked.

"Hi baby, my name is Jane Ann Perry," Mama Jane answered as she opened the door, "but everybody calls me Mama Jane. Come on in. Oh look at those beautiful babies." She said to Kimberly, and hugged her then cooed at Travis and Traniece.

"You can gwawn over there and have a seat next tuh-tuh-tuh . . . I'll get it right directly, chile." Mama Jane laughed.

"Janice." Janice said to Mama Jane.

"That's right, Janice." Mama Jane said as she watched Kimberly sit on the couch, and then returned to the kitchen.

"Hi y'all I'm Chrysta." Chrysta walked out from beyond the living room and announced with a quick smile. "And this is Morgan." A shy and rosy-cheeked Morgan stood a bit closer to Chrysta in the presence of so many unfamiliar faces in the room.

"Hello." Janice and Kimberly said almost in unison. They introduced themselves and their children back to Chrysta and to each other.

"Y'all come on to the table, Janice and Kimberly." Mama Jane said. "Chrysta set up a lil' table for the kids to sit at." She pointed to the short plastic multicolored table with red, blue, orange and green chairs on her way to her own seat.

"Now, everythang's here on the table and Kimberly, I suspect you'll need a hand so hand that baby on over to Mama Jane." Mama Jane said holding her arms open for Traniece.

"Tariq!" Janice said sternly as she caught him out of the corner of her eye taking a toy from Porcha's hands that Morgan had given her.

Mama Jane glanced quickly at Tariq and gave him a grandmotherly look of disapproval.

"Thank you, Mama Jane." Kimberly said handing a playful Traniece to her. They all sat down.

For two hours they laughed, talked, ate, bonded and grew to like one another.

The next day, Kimberly called Mama Jane.

"Mama Jane?" Kimberly said with a pause, noticeably trying to get used to calling her that, rather than Ms. Perry. "Hi this is Kimberly from dinner yesterday. How are you?"

"Oh, hi dahlin'. I'm alright. A little arthur got me this morning but other than that, I'm good. How are you?"

"I am doing well, actually." Kimberly said. "I wanted to tell you how much I enjoyed dinner at your house yesterday. Thank you so much. Also, I just got a call a few minutes ago from Boch Medical Center. They offered me a position that I interviewed for last week and I start the position next week." She said.

"Oh that's good baby." Mama Jane said.

"So, I would like to ask that you keep Traniece and Travis for me when I go back to work. I would feel comfortable with you watching them."

"Oh dahlin', I would love to keep those precious babies." Mama Jane chuckled. "You just bring them right on over here first thing next Monday morning and they'll be just fine."

"Thank you so much Mama Jane. That means so much to me. And please thank Ms. Y at General Oaks for giving me your info the next time that you see her." Kimberly said.

They chatted for a few more minutes about the children and vowed to speak again later on in the week.

# Chapter Six

*Reflect upon your present blessings, of which every man has plenty;*
*not on your past misfortunes, of which all men have some.*

~ Charles Dickens, Novelist

Two months later on a June Sunday afternoon, the neighborhood ice cream truck could be heard a mile away. Janice, Kimberly and their families were now regulars at Mama Jane's Sunday dinners. Tre' had asked his mom that morning if he could take a dollar, one of only two, out of his piggy bank to buy ice cream from the ice cream man. When it finally rolled down Rain Street, Tre', Tariq, Porcha, Morgan and the rest of the neighborhood children were waiting, eagerly and gleefully waving their wrinkled dollars. Travis and Traniece were inside with Mama Jane and Janice and Kimberly had followed the children outside.

"So, how's your job going? Kimberly asked Janice continuing the conversation they started inside.

"It's a job," said Janice.

"I've been out to the Grand Hotel a couple of times and it's beautiful. It must be nice to work in such a beautiful environment." Kimberly told Janice.

"Girl I'm a hotel operator, I wouldn't know about it." Janice laughed. "A shuttle takes us to our employee entrance, we walk an underground tunnel that passes our employee cafeteria, our uniform pick up area, the new employee training room and voila, next thing you know, a set of stairs and we're at the back door of our work area. I've been there for a month now and the last time I saw those beautiful gardens, was the last day of my three day training."

"How was training there?" Kimberly asked.

"Probably not as long as Boch's. I heard y 'all's is intense." Janice said.

Kimberly laughed. "Well, it's a huge hospital and there's so much to learn; booster shots, code black alarms, patient contact, terrorist threats, and hazmat procedures. Not to mention all the little things that goes along with running the admin in a hospital.

She stopped suddenly from her conversation and noticed that something strange was happening with the ice cream truck.

The ice cream man, about a half a block away, stopped. A child walked up to the truck to get some ice cream and was waved away by the ice cream man. A tall man in a black shirt, sagging jeans and black beanie stepped up to the truck and slapped hands with the ice cream man.

Kimberly frowned and looked over at Janice, wondering if she had just seen what transpired.

"Did you see that?" Kimberly whispered to Janice "Yep." Janice said.

The ice cream man finally made his sale to the children he momentarily waved away then slowly began driving towards Janice, Kimberly and the group of children. Their section of apartments were at the end of the block, so it looked as if traffic coming that way, would drive right into their apartment building, therefore it was easy for Janice and Kimberly to see the two men out of their peripheral.

As if in slow motion, while Janice and Kimberly watched the truck approach, they saw two men walking toward each other from opposite sides . . . the thug that just bought drugs from the ice cream man and another man who came from the opposite side of the street from behind a set of bushes. Each man stepped off the sidewalk onto the unusually calm Rains Street. One man stepped off the right sidewalk and the other man stepped off the left sidewalk. Almost in unison, they raised their arms and pointed their weapons toward the back of the tot-chiming rings of the vehicle with the cool summer treats. Janice's eyes widened. She yelled for Porcha and Tariq to get down and rushed to them. Kimberly had already started reaching for Tre' and Morgan and grabbed them and pulled them to the hard concrete. The ice cream man's gaze had been fixed on them. They were right in front of him. So, when he saw them getting to the ground, he slowed the truck down and turned to see what was going on just as the two men began emptying their clips into the back of the truck. The ice cream man caught one in the eye, one in the arm and one in the chest. He fell over backward into the steering wheel as the men continued to walk and fire at the vehicle in rapid succession. The truck wheels turned and it rolled into the curb less than ten feet away from Janice, Kimberly and the kids to a complete stop. The tune continued to play as Janice held Tariq and Porcha and Kimberly held Morgan and Tre' close to them and low to the ground, all of them trembling with fear. Janice uncovered her head slowly to see the thugs had gone into the truck and retrieved the 'trap dope' they had given the pusher ice cream man and ran away.

"It's taking forever for the coroner to get here." Janice said as she stood with Ms. Jane on the street in front of their building, looking over at the ice cream truck across the way. It was three hours later. People had begun passing by to spectate as they heard the news about the body.

"I know," Mama Jane said. "Lawd, Lawd, that's somebody's chile," she said shaking her head with frowned brows, and sighed. She began walking toward her apartment. Pausing, she looked back at Janice, who was still staring at the ice cream man.

"Come on inside, baby, with the rest of us. Let me fix you some tea."

Breaking away from the daze, she followed Mama Jane into her apartment.

Janice sat down at the kitchen table and Mama Jane poured the steaming tea into an old porcelain teacup on a saucer.

Janice sipped while Mama Jane walked back to Morgan's room to check on Kimberly who was sitting with Morgan and Tre' 'til they had joined the twins and fallen asleep. Tariq and Porcha had fallen asleep on Mama Jane's bed.

It was three in the morning and Chrysta was coming home late . . . again. Shirt unbuttoned and lipstick smeared, she went right up to her room in General Oaks and closed her bedroom door. Being out all day, she had missed all of the excitement.

*Knock, knock.* "Chrysta?" Mama Jane said.

Chrysta ran to the mirror and smoothed her hair.

Why is she up?!? Chrysta thought to herself.

"Mama, whatchu doin' up?" she said as she opened the door.

"Chrysta, whatchu doin' just getting home?" Ms. Jane said.

Silence . . .

"I have had your child all day, Chrysta Anne. And she needed you today. You not finna run the streets like these other hot girls round here. You was raised better than that. Can't nothin' godly be goin' on at three in the morning." Mama Jane lectured.

Chrysta turned away to place the brush that she had in her hand on the dresser and rolled her eyes in the process.

"Come sit down and listen to me." Mama Jane said sitting on the side of Chrysta's bed.

Mama Jane told her everything that had happened while she was gone. Chrysta was horrified and asked all the questions she could think of after going in to check on Morgan.

"So, you starting at that new salon tomorrow?" Mama Jane asked when they finished talking about the shooting.

"Yes Ma'am."

"Who is it, your friend's aunt that runs it?"

"Yes ma'am, Shaleathia's aunt Shameka Collins."

"Good. That awda keep you oughta' trouble and from spendin' so much time with that boy."

"What do you mean, Mama Jane? I don't even see him that often. After I get off work, maybe."

"Well, Chrysta, I've said it be foe,' "Mama Jane said, "you gotta use those gifts God gave 'ya. No distractions. Do good at that shop. Give it what I know you can give it." Mama Jane encouraged.

And with that she was on her way back to her room.

Chrysta lay there in her bed after putting on her nightgown. All she could think about was the shooting and how close she was to getting out of General Oaks back in January. She had to get out, and fast.

# Kimberly

It was Monday evening and Kimberly headed home from work to change out of her slacks and blouse into a jogging suit, and then pick the kids up at Mama Jane's.

"Hey, Kimberly can you come over, I need to talk to you." Malik's mother said on the answering machine.

Kimberly called Ms. Mayes back to let her know that she was going to head over after she picked the children up from Mama Jane's.

"Yeah, that's what I wanted to talk to you about," Mrs. Mayes said.

"What do you mean?" Kimberly asked.

"Well, I watched the news yesterday, Kimberly. Don't you think that your dealings up there at General Oaks should have come to an end after that? Don't you think it's dangerous for your children to be there with that woman everyday, all day long?" Mrs. Mayes detailed.

"I'm glad you went into this over the phone," Kimberly responded, "so I wouldn't have to come over to tell you thank you for your concern, but I'll be sticking with the decision that my heart and my budget allowed me to make. Mama Jane is a good woman, she has lived there for twenty years and I believe she would give her life for my children or any of the children that she has practically raised over the past 15 years. They are safe with her."

"Kimberly you have always been too trusting. I think you are making a mistake. This is a different world than the one my son sheltered you in."

"I have to go." Kimberly said after a pause. "Before I say something I'll regret."

She hung up the phone and sat at one of the two bar stools at her small kitchen island. There she let go of the frustrations of the workday, the past few months, and her fears for her future in a nice long cry.

\*     \*     \*

"Hell NAWL, your honor!" Jaurice exclaimed commenting on the figures that the caseworker quoted for what their children needed monthly from him to be properly supported.

Karen stood there with Janice, as promised, and held her hand through the proceedings. Janice had filed for a divorce in February. It was June and the child support hearing this afternoon would be another mark of Janice's new life.

The judge, a large-framed middle-aged woman in her black robe, looked as if she had had enough for the day. She looked Jaurice straight in the eye with her piercing blue eyes and southern drawl and said. "Young man I don't know where you think you are, but you will respect my courtroom."

"She ain't getting' a dime from me—" Jaurice responded and looked over at Janice.

Janice could barely look at Jaurice. She was nauseous and could only think of having a spoonful of starch at that moment.

The judge banged her gavel as snickers poured from the courtroom gallery. "One more outburst and I will hold you in contempt. This state requires that you financially support the children that you have fathered financially and you will do so. It is also ordered that you see your children for visitation every other weekend, two weeks of the summer, two weeks in the winter, and have them on holidays and birthdays, alternating on odd and even years as scheduled according to the state's mandatory parenting plan or your child support will increase. Is that understood? Good." She said without letting Jaurice respond. "It is also ordered that you will pay half of the children's medical bills and if you don't like it, Mr. Walker, I suggest you think twice about fathering more children."

"This is some ole' bullshhii . . . Janice Imma whup yo'—." Jaurice banged his fist on the podium as he glared at Janice and Karen and the caseworker standing next to them.

"—You are in contempt of court . . . bailiff." The judge interrupted, standing up from her chair.

The bailiff came over and restrained Jaurice.

"Hold on bailiff. Madame Court Reporter, did you get that last line?" The judge asked.

"Yes I did your honor." She replied.

"Please read Mr. Walker's parting words back to me." The judge asked, taking a sip of her water.

"This is some bullsh** Janice I'm going to whip your," said the court reporter as if she came straight over from an Ivy League school and sat down to read the latest edition of the Wall Street Journal.

The judge looked at Jaurice, who had been calmed by the tight cuffs the bailiff put on him, and smiled. Letting her smile fade, the judge said, "I'm going to go out on a limb and classify that little show you gave us as a threat. Mr. Walker, show up in my courtroom again and I'll *give you* a show." She quickly put her glasses back on and sat on her bench. "Take him away, bailiff."

"Next case on the docket, please." The judge sighed and adjusted her glasses.

Janice, Karen and the caseworker gathered their belongings and files and walked out of the courtroom.

"Your honor I —." The next man whined as soon as he reached the podium.

"Sir, you don't speak until you are spoken to. If you want to follow in the steps of the last wise guy, by all means, let's skip the formalities and get you back there to join him." Janice heard as she opened the doors to leave.

Silence.

"Fantastic." The judge said going back to reviewing her notes for the case in front of her. "Now . . . ." She began.

In the hallway outside the courtroom doors, Janice was visibly shaking. The overworked case worker noticed.

"Listen, I see cases like yours all the time. I wish it were different for you but I saw his employment record and it looks like he's being evasive. He's going to be hard to track down," Janice listened intensely. "Keep your case active so that when he does decide to work again after having quit this latest job, your children will be in the system to receive their support. I'll warn you, though; it could take months, so do not count on Mr. Walker's consistent assistance. Good luck." And with that, the caseworker took her battered brief case and hurried back into the courtroom leaving Janice standing there in her gray suit from the thrift store specially picked out for the day.

"I'm here your honor." Janice heard the caseworker shout as the courtroom doors swung closed.

Karen walked over to Janice after coming out of the ladies room and gave her a hug. "Come on Sis, let me buy you lunch."

# CHAPTER SEVEN

*We'd never know how high we are till we are called to rise; and*
*then, if we are true to plan, our statures touch the sky.*

~ Emily Dickinson

"Good morning, Chrysta." Shameka greeted.

"Hi Shameka."

"You ready to get started?" she asked.

"I sure am." Chrysta responded.

"Well, for your first day here, I'm going to have you shampoo clients. I want you to get to know them, and I want you to do your best to connect with them. If you have any questions at all, let me know." Shameka instructed.

"Ok, sounds good." Chrysta said with confidence.

Halfway through the day, Chrysta knew that she would love working there. She loved the calm, serene atmosphere of the salon. Massaging client's scalp and listening to the light jazz tickling the speakers was therapy. And it was so different from what she was used to. Most of the clients were professional, working women with spouses and children.

After 10 full hours, Shameka caught Chrysta before she left, told her she had done well, and that she would see her the next day.

At three in the morning, Chrysta couldn't sleep. She took a deep stretch and looked over at her new pre-paid cell phone. It was still on vibrate from working at the salon. Three missed calls. She pulled the cover away from over her legs and slid out of the cool sheets to go and check on Morgan. While walking and flipping through the numbers, she noticed that the last call was from Ced was only moments ago.

"What's up Ced," she whispered peeking in on Morgan who was sound asleep.

"How you do today, shampoo girl?" Ced asked Chrysta.

"I did ah-ight. I think Imma like it there. It's a lot better than those rinky-dink salons I've been working at for the last three years." She replied.

"Ay. Why don't I come 'dat way and we go riding or sumpin.'"

"Now? Where we going?"

"Aw. We can go over to the park and kick it for a minute."

Hesitant she was silent.

"Hallo."

"I'm here." Chrysta said.

"Whazzup? You wanna hook it up or what?"

"Ok," she agreed nonchalantly.

*   *   *

"So I wuhnded to brang you out here to tell you I wanna make you my lady." He said lickin' his lips at Chrysta.

"Yo' lady? Man you don't know nuthin' about me." She added.

"From 'dis day forward you my lady."

*Whatever*, Chrysta thought to herself, propping her feet up on his dash board.

"It's gon' be cool don't you think? N git cho feet down" he said playfully knocking them off the dash."

"I like the single life."

"Girl you ain't never gon' have nobody betta than me."

Chrysta winced and was flattered by the confident overture. In the light that the roof was shining down into the car out of the darkness, she was able to catch a glimpse of Ced's hershey toned shoulders and his rock hard muscular arms in the muscle shirt he was wearing. *He must hit the weights daily to maintain that,* she thought to herself . . . thoroughly impressed.

But Chrysta couldn't ignore the fact that the air was filled with silence. There was no mental chemistry between them. Chrysta wondered how in the world she could be attracted to men that were so completely different.

Chrysta met Morgan's father, Jonathan, after a basketball game she attended with a friend. He was liked by everyone, athletic, smart and she thought she was head over hills in love. However, his parents did not like at all that he was about to become a father before high school ended; the fact that the girl was on the "other side" of the tracks did not help either. He lived in the ritzy side of the city, was an honor roll student, and a member of Jack and Jill. They started hanging out together, but did not date long. Before they knew it, Morgan was conceived in the back of the new Range Rover his parents just bought for him, his choice vehicle for earning a scholarship to college.

"That was the deal," he told her one night as they lay in the blanketed bed of the truck and talked about their families.

"In the ninth grade, they promised me if I got a full four year ride to school they would buy me the car I wanted." He had an air of haughtiness as he told the story to his girl.

After a few more weeks of dating, his parents found out about the pregnancy and offered to pay for an abortion and to put a little change in her pocket. But Chrysta refused.

"Wanna see somthin'?" Ced said in his unmistakable low voice.

"What Ced?" she said as he interrupted her thoughts. She was bored and ready to go home.

He adjusted his pants and fished out his enormous gun.

"What are you doing with that?" Chrysta said.

"I just bought it. Imma keep you safe if you be my lady."

"You just don't give up do you?"

"Hell nawl." He said softly as he leaned over and kissed her neck.

Chrysta was feeling the fact that he wanted to protect her. "Wait a minute . . . . first you gone have to put that gun up."

He quickly placed the gun down under the seat and she smiled and began to kiss him back.

Janice could not sleep either. Out of her window, she saw Chrysta leave with Ced and was still awake when she came back home. Eating spoonfuls of starch, she sat replaying the image over and over again, like a clip from a movie. The nurse came into her exam room to tell her that her pregnancy test was positive. That was weeks ago. No one knew, no one had asked. She was a size sixteen and the clothes that she wore didn't reveal her baby bump much, but she was going to start showing . . . and soon. It was time to deal with the fact that she was now a single mom, living in the ghetto with baby number three on the way.

# CHAPTER EIGHT

*If you can't change your fate, change your attitude.*

~ Amy Tan

It was a little over a week prior to the new school year, and Janice, Kimberly and Chrysta were finding out just how much they had in common. Between Sunday dinners, and picking the kids up everyday from Mama Jane's, they were getting to know one another well.

One thing that they were in agreement about, was that they needed to all be back in school for this fall semester. Chrysta and Kimberly had been told that by Mama Jane and DeMarco respectively, for years. Janice realized she needed to be back too. The last words that Mr. Duke said to her helped to confirm it. And they all felt a sense of urgency for moving on from General Oaks after the ice cream truck incident. They talked it over at Sunday dinner several times.

"Hey I called and spoke to an advisor today at the college." Kimberly told Chrysta as she wheeled around the corner, leaving the parking lot of her job.

"That's good girl! I haven't called up there yet but Imma do it later on today." Chrysta said.

"Ok, you talked to Janice today?" Kimberly asked.

"Uh –uh." I saw her leaving for work this morning though. She looked tired." Chrysta told her.

"I can imagine. It's been a trying few weeks for her." Kimberly said, referring to how tired Janice looked at Sunday dinner a couple of weeks ago when she told them the news about her pregnancy. "I'm going to go by and see if I can do anything to help when I pick the kids up today." Kimberly announced.

"You know, that's a good idea, I'll stop by too. But I probably won't see you, I have a couple of late clients today." Chrysta said.

"Look at you doin' yo' thang!" Kimberly replied.

"I know, right. I just realized that I gotta move myself oughta' here, and not wait for somebody to come and move me out, so I'm permanently focused." Chrysta said.

"I'm scared of you. Well listen, I'll probably talk to you later on tonight if you're not too busy, so we can get together about Janice. Kimberly said.

"Yeah, girl, you can call anytime!" Chrysta replied.

Kimberly drove down 21$^{st}$ Avenue South on the way home from work, and decided to take a different street. She had heard that the city was involved in a revitalization project nearby and she wanted to see what progress was being made. She drove through the tree-lined streets and saw some renovations going on. She was impressed. The modern versions of Victorian styled homes caught her eye immediately. She drove slowly so that she could catch a glimpse of the backyards as well. Most had a deck or an entertaining area in the back. This, along with the bench swings on the front porch, made the homes look family friendly.

Kimberly had always been interested in nice homes. A latch key kid, she finished her teen years in an apartment with her mother and father after they lost their home to a foreclosure when Kimberly was only fourteen. The suburbs, she remembered were different, the big backyards with maple trees, the clean, orderly sidewalks with watchful, protective eyes of middle-aged old women and men. She and Malik were on that path before he died, and she was going to waste no time in getting their family back on track.

After work, Janice picked Tariq and Porcha up from Mama Jane's, and decided that it was time to give Karen the call.

Janice walked in the apartment, tired and with swollen feet. Even though she had not felt like eating dinner, she still participated in her daily ritual . . . two teaspoons of Argo Starch. She had been craving it more and more lately and rewarded herself with an extra scoop.

"Hey Tim, is Karen there?"

"Yeah, Janice, how are ya'?"

"I'm good, thanks. You?"

"Yeah, I'm doing great. Hey let me go and get Karen for ya." Timothy said, sounding busy.

"Hey Sis." Karen announced when she picked up the phone.

"Hey Karen, you got a minute?"

"Yeah baby Sis what's up?"

"Well . . . I'm pregnant."

Silence . . .

"Hello?" Janice asked.

"How far along are you?"

"Oh, Janice. I'm sorry, I wasn't expecting that." Karen replied.

"Five months." Janice answered.

"Five months?" Karen started.

"I didn't want to tell you, so I waited three months to get it together how I was going to tell you, as you can see." Janice explained.

"Does he know?" Karen asked.

"No . . . he doesn't." Janice answered.

"Ok, what can I do to help you?" Karen asked, unsure of what else to say.

"I just wanted you to know. I'm determined to make a life for Tariq and Porcha and me . . . and the baby. I'm sure things are going to get a bit harder before they get easier, so I just need you to keep being my big Sis. I may need a shoulder to cry on." Janice said.

"Well, you know that I'm here if you need me."

"I know." Janice's smile seemed to reach through the phone. "Ok, I gotta go."

"I'll call you tomorrow. Ok?" Karen said.

"Ok, good night." Janice said.

"Night." Karen ended.

Kimberly put everyone to bed with ease that night. Tre' didn't ask for water in order to stay up longer and there was no crying from teething. She was grateful. She pulled out a stack of bills that she had accumulated in a shoebox over the past few months since she had moved into the bungalow.

"No time like the present," she thought. She removed the boxes from underneath the bed and placed them next to her as she sat down just below the pillows. She yawned.

Kimberly opened and categorized every one and fell asleep from mental exhaustion, dreaming about the tree-lined streets that she hoped to move into one day.

Malik enters the room wiping his neck and shoulders with a towel. He slings it down and grabs the lotion from the nightstand, grabs Kimberly's feet and begins to rub the lotion on generously.

"Listen, you have to treat Travis and Tre' a little different than Treniece. You can't yell at 'em. You gotta be tactful."

"Tactful. You mean like the military." She replied.

"Nah. Not like that. You just have to say what you mean . . . lay it down to 'em. And when they don't do it hold 'em accountable. Take away a privilege. No Xbox, no juice. See what I'm sayin'? That way they'll learn not to play you . . . play your soft spot against you. Soon, they'll be young men." Malik stated.

He finishes rubbing her feet and Kimberly ponders what he just said.

"What kind of lotion is that is smells so goo . . ."

In her bed, Kimberly's body darts upwards panting, sweating and breathing out of control. She leaps up and scampers to the bathroom. She cups her hand and immediately starts to down water from the faucet down her throat. Looking in the mirror, she realizes that it was only a dream. Very real, but still a dream. Exiting the bathroom, Kimberly sits on the side of the bed sobbing as she prays to God. Feeling hollow, she longs for her husband who was taken away from her far too soon.

# CHAPTER NINE

*Behold the turtle, He only makes progress when he sticks his neck out.*

~ Tariq Bryant Conant, Educator and Diplomat

On the first night of the semester, Janice and Kimberly were in class together. Since they both were on campus, Chrysta offered to watch Tariq, Porcha, Tre', Travis and Traniece.

"You don't have to do that! I can take them to their grandparents." Kimberly said to Chrysta a week before, when they found out

"Kimberly, why would you drive all the way to the next city and back when I'm a block away. Besides, I talked to Janice earlier, and she said that she has a Thursday class, and so do I, so if we could switch up on watching them, that would work great. Janice is only taking two classes, but she said that she would watch them for a couple of hours every Saturday so we could study."

"Kimberly why don't you just drop the kids off to me. We'll watch 'em for a lil' while." Chrysta stated

"Well, that actually sounds like a great plan. But are you sure that that isn't too many babies in one house for you?"

"I did think about that but with Mama Jane's help, I know I'll make it." Chrysta admitted and laughed.

"Whatchu still doin' up sweet pea?" Chrysta said later that night after she put Traniece and Travis down for bed 'til Kimberly got there.

"No reason," Morgan said combing through the hair of her black Barbie. The four-year old was the spitting image of her father, Chrysta thought.

Chrysta went and sat beside her on her bed.

"Can I paint your nails?" Chrysta asked.

"Yes Ma'am." Morgan lit up like a Christmas tree. She loved seeing her toenails and fingernails painted like the "big girls" on television.

Chrysta walked across the hallway, went into her tiny bedroom and pulled out her palest pink nail polish.

"Here we go." She said walking back into the room and holding it up in the air for Morgan.

"Hey Porcha," Chrysta said after being startled, finding the little girl standing behind her rubbing her eyes.

"I thought you were asleep"

"Nawl," she said in her deep raspy voice. "I ain't sleep. Whatcha'll doin?" Porcha asked.

"We're just painting our nails, want to come join us?" Chrysta smiled at her.

Porcha widened her eyes, and nodded her head so hard it seemed as if it were disconnected from her shoulders.

"Come sit beside me." Morgan said.

Chrysta was pleased that Morgan was sharing and being so polite. She had never had other kids around consistently before Janice and Kimberly came and with Chrysta not being able to afford day care, she stayed home with Mama Jane every day and Chrysta worried that she would be spoiled or introverted. She was neither.

The next three months flew by with Janice, Kimberly and Chrysta sharing the babysitting duties for class, and study time seamlessly. But the first Thursday night of October, that all changed. Janice passed Chrysta a note in class that simply read:

"Contractions!"

Chrysta and Janice quietly walked out of class and headed for the hospital with Chrysta making calls all the way there.

Kimberly showed up thirty minutes later.

"Where are the kids, Kimberly?" Chrysta asked, surprised to see her.

"DeMarco and his date came by the house and told me it was cool to come, and they would stay and put the kids to bed."

\*   \*   \*

# First week in October

"AHHHH!!!" Janice bellowed at 3am in the morning to the top of her lungs.

"Push, Janice, push!" Janice had Kimberly's hand on one side and Chrysta's on the other.

"Doctor, the baby is crowning." The nurse routinely told the doctor as he washed his hands.

"What kind of old book did you read, that convinced you not to get that needle put in your back to get rid of this pain, Janice?" Chrysta asked.

"I went with Kimberly to the library, they had . . . Ahhhh Eeeeesh!" Janice attempted to tell her.

"She didn't mean answer the question, girl, PUSH!" Kimberly cited.

During the last few weeks of Janice's pregnancy, Chrysta and Kimberly had really been there for her. They had taken care of Tariq and Porcha when she was tired and could not. They even accompanied her to a free Lamaze class at the Metro clinic for low income women; a week after that, she told them that she really wanted them to be in the delivery room with her to usher her new baby into the world.

Ahhhh!!!! Janice yelled.

The stench of alcohol in the cold, fluorescent lit room made Janice shiver with anticipation.

"Ok, Janice. I'm going to count to ten. When I begin at one, I want you to bear down for all ten counts." Instructed the doctor. "Do not stop pushing 'til I get to ten, ok?"

"One," he began, "nine, ten. Good job." He said. Janice grunted.

"Good Janice, now rest a minute." The doctor said patting her on her stirruped leg. "Ok, Janice, we're about to do it again . . . a couple more pushes and your son will be here. Hummm." He said eyeing her vaginal area.

Rolling backward away from Janice, he gave the nurse a look of concern, then he whispered slightly toward her direction . . . "Heather, get me the forceps . . . we're going to have to help the baby come through. It must be a big one."

"Ok, Janice, the baby's head is almost out. So, on my count, I want you to start pushing again just like before, ok . . . One, two, three, five, and six, keep pushing, keep pushing eight . . ."

"Niye, ten . . . you did awagin." a garbled voice mumbled. The room was suddenly filled with the foul stench of stale bourbon mixed with malt liquor and broasted chicken as suddenly, a drunken Jaurice stumbled in the room. He was carrying a liquor bottle in one hand and a greasy white bag in the other sucking on a chicken bone.

"If you thank Immo pay for another baby you out yo damn mind. Dey already taking half my check right nah." Jaurice yelled furiously as he rocked from side to side in a stupor.

"Sir. You must leave here, now." The doctor ordered. "Heather call security."

"Jaurice, pleeeeeeeeeeeease! Ohhhhhhhhh!." Janice yelped.

Kimberly leaped to the doorway. "Umm. Jaurice now's not the time for this. We'll work this out later."

"Get off me! You on't know me." He barked.

"Ma'am who is that guy." The doctor asked Kimberly.

"Ummm. That is the father." Kimberly retorted, walking back over to Janice.

"Yeah. Ida daddy. Jaurice yelled.

"I'll call security, again." Heather, the nurse stated as she snatched the phone from the table.

"I'yahhh." Janice screamed.

"Push!" The doctor yelled.

Jaurice screaming and half-crying said, "You takin' all my money. Sickuv it. You hear me. YOU HEAR ME?" He cried. Jaurice then hurled the liquor bottle at Janice's head. The bottled shattered above the wall and a piece of glass knicked her on the forehead.

"Owwwwwwwwwwwww!" Janice exclaimed.

Moments later, three burly security officers encircled an intoxicated Jaurice and physically wrestled him to the ground and placed handcuffs on his wrist. Chrysta scampered out of the way for her own safety. They hoisted him up and led him down the bright lights of the hallway as hospital workers looked on in disbelief. Jaurice continued to rant about money as his yells got fainter.

One nurse picked up the glass from under the bed, and another nurse tended to the small gash on her forehead dabbing it with alcohol and placing a small bandage over the wound.

"You're gonna be fine." The nurse stated.

"Now, let's get our baby." The doctor announced. "one, two, three, four . . ."

The doctor used the forceps to help pull the baby's head out and grabbed the baby's shoulders with both hands twisting him and turning him until the rest of his body flailed in the air unconfined "and oohhhhhh! It's a boy!"

"Ahhhh" . . . Janice groaned loudly in relief.

Janice looked up at Kimberly briefly still holding her hand and received a smile and a wink . . . "good job mom."

"You ok Sweetie? You want some ice chips?" Chrysta asked nervously. "Whooo, I never seen it from those angles before!"

"Ten fingers and ten toes . . . . I counted." Kimberly smiled as she patted Janice's sweaty forehead with a cloth.

"Nine pounds and nine ounces, doctor." Nurse Heather proclaimed as the doctor was finishing all of the post-labor procedures with Janice.

"Whewww!" the doctor exclaimed. "That's what I call a bouncing baby boy! I can honestly say that I've never been on a delivery this exciting before. It's the stuff movies are made of."

"Well, Sweetie . . . what is his name?" Kimberly asked.

"I named him Joshua . . . it means . . . 'God rescues.'"

"Ain't that the gospel truth?" Kimberly quipped.

Later that evening, Janice had slept, fed baby Joshua for the first time, and she, Chrysta and Kimberly had dressed him for his first picture. "Hey Mama Jane!" Janice smiled as she sighted Mama Jane coming through her hospital room door later. She was elated to see Mama Jane. Chrysta and Kimberly had gone home to get all of the children ready for school. Aunt Gigi and Karen had come by earlier.

"Hey Shugah" Mama Jane said as she walked through the hospital room door over to her and taking her hand.

"Chile, I saw that big ole boy down the hall!" Mama Jane chided. "You did real good." She said smoothing her hair back, and kissing her forehead. She had grown to be just like one of her own over the past few months.

"Thank you for coming." Janice said as a tear fell. Both she and Mama Jane knew what the emotions were about without her having to say a word. She has another baby in a household that she is barely able to make ends meet in. Mama Jane understood and comforted, "It doesn't matter where we've been, chile, it matters where we plan to take ourselves."

That evening, courtesy of the state's insurance plan, Janice and Joshua were sent home.

# CHAPTER TEN

*Every achiever that I have ever met says, 'My life turned around when I began to believe in me'.*

~ Dr. Robert Schuller, Minister and Author

"Hey Shoogah." Mama Jane said the next day as she walked through the hospital room door over to Janice and took her hand. "Chile, I saw that big ole boy down the hall!" Mama Jane chided. "You did real good," she said smoothing her hair back and kissing her forehead as if she were her own daughter.

"Mama Jane," Janice said in more of a somber mood than yesterday. "I don't know if I did the right thing. I feel like I am the last person that oughta' have a baby right now livin' where I'm livin', makin' what I'm makin'—and the baby's daddy don't even know he exists."

Mama Jane motioned for Chrysta to pull up a chair for her to sit in. Mama Jane sat down and took Janice's hand.

"Listen to me. You did do the right thing. Look at how you are changing your life. You're so much different from the way you were when I met you almost a year ago." Mama Jane said with Chrysta nodding in agreement. "You are doing right by getting yourself together fo' your churrens and you oughta' never ever feel bad about that!"

"True." Chrysta said thinking of how Mama Jane has been telling her the same thing over the past few months.

"You gonna be just fine," she shook Janice's hand in hers as Janice let a tear fall. "Immo make shoal of it."

Chrysta and Mama Jane visited with Janice for a few more minutes before leaving.

On their way out of the hospital, they passed Karen and spoke with her for a few minutes. She told them that she was there to take Janice home, and that she would be spending a couple of days with her. And even though they'd only spoken a couple of times, she wanted to thank them for everything that they were doing for her little sister. She gave them a big hug and continued to Janice's room with a large stuffed animal and flowers.

The next week, Janice was home and Chrysta and Kimberly went by to visit her.

Tariq opened the door, and dressed in her fiercest party clothes, Chrysta walked in wearing a sparkling tank top, a short mini skirt with leggings, 4-inch heels and a camel coat. Kimberly walked in a few steps behind her, but had to run to catch up until she got to the metal screen door.

"Look at Chrysta in her shiny shine. Shining and blingin', just like the North Star leading the slaves." Janice said.

"Ha! Be quiet." Chrysta laughingly quipped.

"Where are you going?" Janice said struggling to raise herself in the bed to talk with them.

"That's what I wanna know." Kimberly joined in, and then looked over into the bassinet next to Janice's bed. Joshua was peacefully sleeping.

"Well, seeing how Ced and I are no longer together, I'm back out there." Chrysta said consciously trying to lift her head.

"Wha??? What happened, girl?" Janice asked. "Hand me that starch o'er there, Kim." Janice said to Kimberly almost in a whisper while they waited for Chrysta to explain.

"Girl, please." Chrysta answered. "Must I start singing the Scrubs song up in here? As much as he was trying to pick me up before and after work, which was sweet, I needed him to go to his own job. A job, that never existed."

"Right, sweet is not the equivalent of gainfully employed." Kimberly nodded.

"But here's the thing, it wasn't a bad break up." Chrysta explained. "I mean he wasn't horrible to me or anything, I just want more and he's just kinda satisfied with living at home with his Mama and not workin'."

"So, we're out to replace him so soon . . . like tonight?" Janice asked.

"To be honest I want to be out on my own, stable at the salon, and almost finished with school before I get serious about another dude."

Chrysta said folding some of the baby's clothes she saw lying on the bed. "I noticed with the women at the salon, that they don't have alotta drama. The stuff they talk about is not like, *I can't get him to go to work* or *me and my man got into a fight last night.*"

Janice looked down and rubbed the back of her head.

"Everybody gets into fights every now and again." Kimberly said.

"I'm talkin' about fist fights Kimberly, not arguments. See you don't know nothing about 'dat, girl." Chrysta said rubbing her back. "I'm talkin' bout, when a dude is choking you and you pick up an iron and hit him on the head with it, and then he just start landing left and right hooks on you like you anotha dude. That's the stuff I grew up with. That's what I saw growing up in General Oaks every single weekend, cops pulling up with sirens on a," she raised her fingers in air quotes, "'domestic situation.'"

"So, why you dressin' up tonight then?" Janice asked, trying to get off the subject.

"Well, while all that climbing up the ladder is going on, a girl's still gonna have needs." Chrysta said and raised her left brow.

Janice and Kimberly both shook their heads at the youngest member of their group. "Be super careful with that." Kimberly said.

"Yeah." Janice said, looking over at Joshua.

"Enough about me, how are you feeling, Janice?" Chrysta asked.

"Like I've been hit by a Mack truck, but as usual you've taken my mind off of it with one of your stories." Janice smiled at her.

"And you shouldn't be the only one with stories, when are you going on a date Kimberly?" Janice asked cautiously not knowing if she would be offended since it had only been a year since Malik's death.

"Girl, 'The Tiger' won't let me go out." Kimberly laughed it off, slightly uncomfortable.

"Girl you kill me talkin' bout 'The Tiger', what he do today?" Janice asked.

Chrysta laughed.

"You know he had me running all over campus . . . as usual. He ain't happy 'til he sees me working my fingers to the bone and going home falling in the bed asleep. I ain't got time for nothing else BUT Tre', Traniece, Travis and 'The Tiger.'"

They all laugh.

*     *     *

"You got yo' glad rags on don't you? Where you goin'?" Mama Jane asked Chrysta an hour after she and Kimberly left Janice's apartment.

"To the club, Mama Jane." Chrysta answered smiling.

Chrysta kissed Mama Jane on the cheek, went back into the bathroom to check her lipstick one more time, kissed Morgan good night and was out the door.

As Chrysta hurriedly pulled into the parking lot to meet two of her co-workers from the salon, a dark late model car with tinted windows slowly pulled up next to her. Chrysta got out of Mama Jane's Cutlass, carrying her clutch and ran in to meet her friends.

# 3:50 AM

General Oaks was largely asleep in the wee hours of Sunday morning. One or two winos were stumbling around from their last call of the cheapest wines from the corner liquor store purchased earlier in the night.

Chrysta let herself in and looked in on Morgan and Mama Jane. They were both peacefully asleep in their rooms. Chrysta walked to her room and quickly fell asleep across her bed with her clothes on.

BOOOOOM, BOOOOOM, BLAAAP. Twenty minutes later, the front door was smashed in by black dusty Reeboks. Three slender built men wearing all black with ski masks on, flew through the obliterated entrance and headed for the bedrooms.

Mama Jane was awakened. "Chrysta is that you makin' all 'dat racket?" She inquired, jolted from her deep sleep.

One of the men jumped straight into her room.

"Shut up, ole lady!" He barked in a vehement snarl and struck her with a small tree branch.

"Oooooh!" She yelped in pain and fear. The man threw open her chest of drawers and began to ransack them looking for valuables.

"Jack Pot!" he called to the other misfits, referring to Mama Jane's secret stash. The other two men headed through the rest of the house pilfering through the main items of furniture.

The enforcer that struck Mama Jane went to the back bedroom. By this time, Chrysta was up; terrified and confused. The man bolted through the door wasting no time.

"Give it all up hoe." He pronounced.

Chrysta screamed in fright wriggling her legs wildly on the bed. "I don't have nothin."

The man scanned the room intensely. Still holding her down with the tree branch, he went over Chrysta's clutch and emptied it with one hand while holding the stick with the other hand. The only things that fell out were a comb, tube of lip gloss and a condom.

"Dis ain't cho guyt-damn day." The man then began to beat Chrysta on her back and shoulders with the stick while she yelled and did her best to deflect the varied blows to her body.

Then, Morgan's door creaked open. "Mommy! What's wrong?"

The other two men began to approach Morgan's room and Chrysta flipped. She managed to get free; grabbed the large, heavy hot comb she kept on her dresser and smashed the enforcer's head with it. He stumbled over and she slung the device at the other two men. Struggling to get to her daughter and protect her, she then grabbed some air freshener from her dresser and sprayed the men directly in the eyes as they came toward them. They began to cough and scurry back towards the door. One of the men managed to kick her in the stomach in the chaos, and Chrysta shrieked in pain but rage enveloped her. She pushed Morgan into her room and shut the door with a loud bang but could still hear Morgan crying loudly. Mama Jane was unconscious. Chrysta headed straight for the kitchen to get the .38 revolver Mama Jane kept for many years in the last cabinet on the right. She ran away from the men and arrived in the kitchen and opened the cabinet. It wasn't there.

"Let's roll up oughta' here." The enforcer commanded the other two men as they all came to themselves at roughly the same time.

The men were approaching Chrysta in the kitchen, to deal a final fury of blows to the twenty-one year old.

Seeing them coming for her out of the corner of her eye, she turned one final time and felt a stack of newspapers in the cabinet nearby where the pistol used to be. They were coming for her, all three of them and she had to find it. She reached underneath the papers and felt the cold grip of its black handle. She could smell the cologne and hear their footsteps getting closer and closer. Pistol in hand, she turned away from the cabinet, barely gripping the gun tight and in one fluid motion aimed and released the bullet.

"Pop, pop!" The gun sounded as Chrysta gave the enforcer two in the shoulder. He grabbed it in writhing pain as blood shot out spilling on the floor. Then all three men broke and ran for the entrance. Chrysta shot another round aiming at one of their heads but missed.

The attackers headed into the night disappearing into the woods adjacent to the interstate one block from the projects.

Chrysta placed the gun down. "Morgan! Mama Jane!" Chrysta screamed in fear, running to their bedrooms.

At the hospital, Chrsyta and Morgan sat next to the hospital bed as Mama Jane lay there, her head wrapped in a bandage.

"The doctor said you have some pretty extensive injuries, but you gonna be all right." Chrysta said, finally calm.

Mama Jane responded faintly and out of sorts, "The only docta' I listen to is my Docta' Jesus."

Chrysta smiled and whispered. "Always giving HIM the glory in the good and the bad." She kissed Mama Jane on the forehead.

"Is my baby okay?" Mama Jane asked as she came to.

"I'm okay." Morgan replied sadly.

"Chrysta, how did them folk get in the house?"

"They broke in."

Kimberly crashed into the emergency room. "Oh my God. Is she okay?" she asked.

"She's gonna be okay." Chrysta announced.

"Janice called and told me she saw you, but couldn't catch you before you left with the ambulance. I'm sorry Chrys . . . is there something I can do?" Kimberly asked.

"Thank you for being here." Chrysta replied softly with tears in her eyes and gave Kimberly a hug.

"Where are the kids?" Chrysta asked.

"Oh, they're with Malik's parents this weekend. They wanted to give me a little break." She said frowning, still concerned for her friend.

A young white police detective dressed in a blue blazer and khakis walked in and greeted the others. He gave a serious look at Momma Jane.

"Miss Perry, I'm Detective Rhinehart. We were able to track down the suspects after a patrol car spotted three suspicious men in a vehicle about three miles north of General Oaks. One of them had been shot in the shoulder. We just wanted to let you know we got them." Detective Rhinehart stated.

"Who were they?" Kimberly asked.

The detective checked his notes. "Looks like they were part of a little loose band of thugs—they call themselves theeee-yah . . ." he said trying to make out the written note. "The Grey Goose Boys. The perps names were Warren Williams, Tariq McCoy and Cedric Henderson." Recognizing Cedric Henderson as her latest lover, Ced, Chrysta dropped her head in shame. *I'm responsible for this mess*, she thought. I gotta get our money back if it's the last thing I do. "Williams was the one that was shot." The officer added.

Chrysta stood up, and walked out of the room with Kimberly following closely behind her. She walked all the way to the end of the hall toward the window that framed the city's downtown.

"I gotta get us oughta' there." she cried as she turned around.

Kimberly hugged her, and Chrysta leaned on her shoulder and cried louder, "I gotta get us oughta' there!"

# CHAPTER ELEVEN

*People of mediocre ability sometimes achieve outstanding success because they don't know when to quit. Most men succeed because they are determined to.*

~ George E. Allen

It had been over six months since the incident in the delivery room, and Jaurice had not seen his children. Janice had not heard from him since the court date about visitation, and of course she had received no child support from him either. The child support office said he was either not working, or his work was undocumented, and there was nothing they could do but wait.

That is why she was surprised when she heard a knock at her door, and when she looked through her peephole, found Jaurice standing there.

Through the peephole she said, "I don't know what you want but I'm not about to let you in."

"Janice, I just want to talk to you." He sighed in frustration and took his baseball cap off his head. He was looking around and checking out the place it seemed.

"There's nothing to talk about." Janice responded.

"I think there is." He said and looked straight into the peephole.

She was nervous and tense but just as she had practiced with her mentor, she said, "Jaurice, you can't just show up at my house like this. If you wanna talk we can, but it has to be a time and place both of us agree to."

Silence.

Janice went on, "I can meet you next Thursday at five at the Starbucks on West End." Planned time, public place, lots of eyes. She gave herself a mental pat on the back. Janice could barely walk, but was due to be back in her class next Thursday. So since she was going to have a sitter, she thought she might as well get this over with before she went to class.

She peeped through the peephole, and saw Jaurice's jaw line tighten and then bite his lip. An "Ah-ight" escaped his voice and came through the door without a trace of anger or frustration. "I'll see you next week."

Jaurice put his hat back on, turned around and walked to his car.

Janice took a deep breath, backed up and walked to the kitchen. She took the burgundy, near empty box of starch out of the cabinet, and stuffed two spoons full down her throat back to back as she replayed what had just happened. Quickly, she picked up her phone and dialed Karen's phone number.

*       *       *

The choir was singing a modern version of *Oh Happy Day* when Kimberly entered the sanctuary for the late service. She had not been to church consistently since Malik's death, but she definitely felt that she needed to get back to that place in her life. It was missing and she felt the emptiness.

She walked into the mega church's spacious open foyer, that boasted of a three leveled auditorium, and a grand central staircase leading up to each of them. There were also sets of stairs on the opposite sides near the exits, as well as two sets of elevators on the other sides of the church bookstore. A smiling usher led her to her seat as she walked the carpeted slope down toward the pulpit. The usher seated her close to the front as the choir sang what was probably just their second or third selection.

As Kimberly sat through the message entitled "Letting Go of the Past and Reaching Forward to God", she let the tears fall. She vowed to let go of the past, and she made a commitment to focus more on Him.

*       *       *

Chrysta's back and shoulders were still badly bruised from the beating she took during the break-in. She carefully helped Mama Jane inside the apartment. Other than a few headaches, Mama Jane had told everyone she was back to normal and 'kickin' in high gear'.

"Mama Jane, sit here on the couch and put your feet up." Chrysta said as the house phone rang.

"Chrysta, this is Ginger over at the salon. I've been trying to reach you but your cell's voicemail is full. Anyway, I'm sorry to hear about what happened, but if you're feeling better at all, we need you over here. Shameka put that new ad on the radio, and we have just been inundated with new clients . . . a lot more than she forecasted. It's a good thing, but we want them to feel like we're ready for them, even though we're not," the fast talking stylist said, not taking a breath. "So Shameka wanted me to give you a call, to see if you were up to stepping up as a stylist starting today. What do ya say?"

Chrysta tried not to scream from excitement and said, "I'll be right in Ginger!" Chrysta hung up the phone.

"Mama Jane, I—"

"I heard the whole thing dahlin', go. Go on now. I'll take care of Morgan."

"Actually, I was going to take her to Janice's. She said she would keep her if you needed any rest and I needed to go anywhere."

"I'm alright I tole ya. You get on to that shop. That's your destiny, chile."

And with that, Chrysta kissed Mama Jane on the cheek in appreciation, and was out the door.

\*    \*    \*

After church, Kimberly took advantage of her time alone, and drove south listening to the smooth jazz of 88.1 WFSK until the city skyline disappeared out of her rearview. The city's annual Parade of Homes was the place to check out the hottest new trends in the real estate/construction industry. Five new construction homes aligned the street, and each of their windows reflected the setting sun. All of them boasted of the city's most talented builders and designers work.

Kimberly slowly walked up the hardwood stairs of the first house, sliding her fingers along the wood-grained railing as she climbed. The jingling of her bracelets was the only noise that could be heard on the west wing, since there were only a few families on the grounds that last evening of showing. It was not hard for her to imagine living in the home overlooking the lake in the back yard.

She envisioned herself pulling into the three car garage, strutting up the steps into the mud room, checking the laundry chute across the hall to see how many clothes had piled up during the week. Then she saw herself strolling into the large, spacious, open great room, boasting of old teak wood beams in the vaulted ceiling with the kitchen combination and huge black and grey speckled granite-top island. In the gourmet kitchen, she'd take a pack of chicken breasts out of the stainless steel double doors bottom freezer, to thaw for dinner that night.

She dreamed about walking into her enormous master suite, and stepping out of her heels onto the plush cream carpet with a California King that sat firmly in the middle of the room. A few steps away from the two sitting chairs and table that glowed with soft light in the evening, and reflected the waterfall nearby on the other side of the patio. She would walk into her master bath that was as large as her current bedroom, and wash her hands in one of the sinks in the double vanity bathroom. She grabbed the remote on her nightstand, sat on her lavish bed and queued up the concealed fifty two inch LED to rise from the floor near the footboard, as it did, it hid the bedroom's stone fireplace and she watched a bit of CNN for a moment while she balanced her checkbook.

After changing into her spandex workout gear, she pressed another button and fifty-two inches would descend back into the floor. She would then leave the master retreat through the same small hallway, and up the same wood grain stair case she is now walking up to check the children's rooms. They would be at school and daycare this morning, but she would check the closets in their aviation, basketball and Pocahontas themed rooms to make sure that clothes were clean and on hangers. She would check the Jack and Jill bathrooms, to make sure that they were clean and didn't need any soap, toothpaste, lotion or other toiletries.

Leaving the spacious warm atmosphere of the children's rooms, she would head downstairs using the back staircase past the main floor, down to the basement with the theater room and gym complete with an equipped yoga studio. After putting in a couple of miles on the treadmill, she would shower in the master bath, grab a cup of yogurt and walk on the hardwood floors through the gorgeous space toward the massive front door into the office on the right, across from the large formal dining room.

Waking up from that day dream was difficult but Kimberly did. She walked through the other four properties with just as much passion. She took notes, and took particular notice of the black baseboards, soft lighting fixtures, and etcetera. By the time she started her car to journey back into the city, the sun had performed its disappearing act and she had seven and a half pages of notes.

\*    \*    \*

That Thursday, Chrysta and Janice pulled up to leave the children with Kimberly and they pulled up at the same time. Janice had talked to Chrysta and Kimberly about her meeting earlier that week.

"Are you sure you don't want me to roll with you?" Chrysta asked as they each got out of their cars to walk up to Kimberly's house.

"My sister Karen asked me the same thing, and so did her husband." Kimberly had walked out to meet them in time to hear them talking. "But I think it'll be fine. That's why I told him to meet me at Starbucks, since it's public place."

"That was a smart move Janice." Kimberly said.

"Yes it was." Chrysta agreed. "Mama Jane was right. You are doing the right things to change your life, girl."

"Well, I have had a lot of help along the way. As a matter of fact, if my brother-in-law had not found this car for me at an auction," She turned and pointed to the 1995 Toyota Corolla. "I wouldn't even have a way to get over there."

## Baby crying in the back ground.

"Oh, y'all gotta go, Joshua's crying." Kimberly said. "Give him to me and I'll get him settled inside."

She made sucking noises on his cheeks, and he quieted down while she threw his baby bag over her shoulder and walked inside.

"Ok, Chrysta I'll see you in class." Janice said walking behind Kimberly to see them inside.

"Ok, bye." Chrysta said waving to Morgan as she ran in to see her friends.

\*    \*    \*

Janice sat at Starbucks nervously sipping her tea.

Jaurice walked over to Janice's table and she stared coldly into his eyes, just like she had practiced in the mirror all week. She had to admit that he looked better than he ever had, she just could not keep her mind from wandering. Fresh goatee and thick waves on his head; the deepening of his dimples every time he chewed on his toothpick had her replaying memories.

*Snap out of it!* She said to herself. *This man is no good for you. You have finally escaped.*

"What is it that you want to talk about Jaurice? And make it quick. I don't have a lot of time."

"Ok," he said. He leaned over the table and took the toothpick out of his mouth. "I got another son."

"And?" Janice asked not flinching.

"And? Whaaduya mean and?" Jaurice pulled back and questioned.

". . . Another son you can ignore like Tariq, another one you can smoke in front of, drank in front of, hit me in front of?"

Jaurice licked his lips and looked at Janice convincingly, "I am sorry for all I put you through, okay? It's been hell without you. I-I-I-I mean it Janice, I need you." He stuttered.

Despite everything in her that wanted to wrap her arms around him, and tell him she's missed him because he's all she's known. She thought of what Mama Jane said to her, she thought of her babies crying, witnessing every fight they had, thought of Mr. Duke, Karen, Chrysta and Kimberly and she stood, grabbed her purse and walked away without a word, leaving him sitting there.

"Janice. AY! Janice!" Jaurice called after her.

He slammed his fist on the Starbucks table and Janice slightly jumped at the sound. She looked to the side to see the other patrons had turned their heads to look at him momentarily, but said nothing. She kept walking until she was in the car and then drove safely away.

# CHAPTER TWELVE

*Nurture your dreams, Discover your passion, Embrace your visions, Free your spirit, Share your love, Love your soul.*

~ Vicki Virk

On the way home from her first night of class in the new semester, Chrysta heard a noise coming from the engine of the old Cutlass and pulled over.

"*What is that?*" she whispered to herself getting out of the car.

She popped the hood and walked around to open it.

A man pulled up behind her in a late model Chevy. The tall man with toffee brown skin, got out of his truck and slowly walked over to Chrysta, then introduced himself.

"Hey, my name is Jesse." He extended his hand out to shake Chrysta's hand. "I've seen you around in General Oaks where my mother lives."

"I'm Chrysta." She said giving him the once over as discreetly as she could.

"What's wrong with your car?" Jesse frowned a little.

"Well, it's my grandmother's car, and its old so there's no telling what's wrong with it," she said.

"Mind if I take a look?" Jesse asked"

"Go ahead." Chrysta stepped back and watched the man in brown boots and baggy jeans try to assess the problem with Mama Jane's car. She stood aside while he moved from under the hood to the driver's seat to try to start it and back again.

Jesse raised himself up from under the hood on his third trip with a somber look on his face and said, "I think it's your alternator."

"What? Can an alternator just go out like that? I didn't even get a warning." Chrysta said. "Ugh."

"Yeah, that happens sometimes, especially with older cars, but it can be fixed and back on the road this week. But listen, if you want, I will take you back to General Oaks."

Chrysta hesitated, remembering what happened the last time she let a man give her a ride.

Sensing her uneasiness, he said, "Or you can use my phone to call somebody to come get you?"

"I have a phone, but thanks."

"Listen, it's getting cool out here, so why don't you make your call from my car while I look under the hood some more."

"Okay, thanks."

Chrysta walked over to Jesse's car, and he opened the passenger side door for her. Chrysta slid inside the warm leather seats. He closed her door and walked back over to the Cutlass to take one last look under the hood again.

Chrysta watched him walk away, as the CD player in the truck softly played Jamie Foxx's *DJ Play a Love Song*. She pulled out her phone and called Kimberly to ask her to come and get her. By the time she hung up, Jesse was walking back toward the truck.

"Did you make your call?" He asked as he slid in the driver's seat.

"Yeah, I got somebody on the way." Chrysta said, thankful.

"Cool. You know. You did my Mama's hair a few weeks ago and she can't stop talkin' 'bout you."

"Ummm . . . what's her name?" She asked.

"Polly Mae Smith," he answered.

"Oh, Ms. Smith." She said with recognition. "She's a sweetheart."

"Yeah, if I'm taking her to the grocery store or something and she sees you, she always points you out to me." Jesse's gaze shifted away from Chrysta to the floor of his truck, then back up into Chrysta's eyes. "From what I've seen of my mom when she leaves your shop, it's clear to see that you got skills. And if you don't mind me saying so, you are beautiful." Chrysta gazed back at Jesse.

"Well. Thanks." Chrysta was feeling a bit awkward. "Ya know there is a Family Dollar over there and I have some things to pick up, so I'm going to kill two birds with one stone and shop while I wait for my ride."

"Whatcha gone do about the car?" Jesse asked. "Your insurance going to come get it?"

"I've just got liability on it. I have some cousins that I think will take care of it for me. I don't know if they can get to it tonight though."

"Hummmm..." Jesse contemplated. "One of my boys owns a tow truck. I can get him to tow it to your mechanic for you tonight if you want. I just got off the phone with him and I know he is not busy right now."

"Ya' think?" Chrysta asked.

"For sure." He replied.

"But I don't have enough money for a tow tonight. I'll wait on my cousins' tomorrow."

"Oh no, it's okay. I'll take care of it. And he's a friend so he won't charge me full price anyway." He said chuckling.

"You just an all-around resource center, ain't ya?' Chrysta remarked flirtatiously.

"In my spare time, I'm an MMA fighter."

"MMA. What is that?" Chrysta asked.

"Mixed Martial Arts."

"You mean like Wha-chi, Jet Li stuff?" She asked.

"Sumpin' like that." Jesse answered.

"Sounds exciting." Chrysta replied.

Kimberly arrived fifteen minutes later to pick Chrysta up and when she walked out of the store, she noticed that Jesse was still there.

He walked over to her.

"You're still here?" She questioned.

"Yeah, I wanted to make sure you got picked up alright and . . ." he smiled, "you forgot to give me your keys."

"Oh," Chrysta tilted her head back and laughed.

Chrysta gave Jesse the keys to the Cutlass and said, "Here you go, the keys to the Bentley. If it gets lost, I know where yo' Mama lives." Chrysta said jokingly.

Jesse winked at her and said "Yes, ma'am."

Chrysta turned and walked away to get in the car with Kimberly.

Jesse held his gaze on Chrysta as she left, clenched his jaw and got back in his truck to call his friend with the tow truck.

"What was that, girl?" Kimberly asked as Chrysta got into the car.

She looked over at Kimberly and said, "Nothin.'" With a sheepish grin as they drove away.

*     *     *

Later that night, Kimberly tiptoed around the house barefoot, finishing the last of her evening chores. She packed the twins' bags for Mama Jane's, and packed a lunch for herself and Tre for school the next day. As she worked, LeToya Luckett's *Torn* played from the kitchen counter radio. She peeked in on the twins to make sure they were sleeping and the closer she got to the room, she heard that at least one of them was awake. When she entered the room, she saw Travis crawling around in the crib looking at the toys attached. Just beyond his crib, was the window that she could see General Oaks from far in the distance. She watched the two police cars speed up the hill, but faintly heard their sirens. *Another day in the neighborhood*, she whispered to herself.

She walked over to the shades, closed them tighter and picked her baby up out of his crib to rock him back to sleep.

*     *     *

Janice sat on her bed eating her daily ration of starch, and listening to Mary J. Blige's *What's The 411?* album. She was about to turn her light off to go to sleep when Tariq came to her door.

"Mamma, where Deddy at?" He asked.

"Wow, this is out of the blue, Tariq. What made you wanna ask about your daddy?" She said, putting everything aside as he sat on the bed.

"I dunno. I ain't seen him in a long time." He responded.

"Well, Mom and Dad did not get along too well, and so we're just not together anymore."

"So you made him go away." Tariq said, as his voice rose.

"No Tariq, I didn't say that." It was hard not to yell to the top of her lungs *your father is a no good bastard who doesn't know how to treat a woman and I can't tell you how much he hurt me,* but did exactly as she was taught at the shelter for abused women and gave a politically correct answer. "I said that we did not get along, Tariq."

Tariq stood in the middle of the floor with a pained and angered look on his face, arms folded tightly, he began to cry. "You did make him go away and he don' won't me do he? Do he Mama, Deddy don't want me!" Tariq yelled and grunted through his tears.

"Oh baby, I love you." Janice said to Tariq. She got off the bed and rushed over to him with tears in her eyes. She bent down to hug him and took his seven-year old body tightly in her grasp, and held him like she would never let go. As Tariq cried into his mother's chest, Janice closed her own eyes and let a tear fall for her baby boy.

*   *   *

The next evening, Chrysta was dropped off from work by a co-worker and was just in time to read Morgan a story before bed. She then lay in bed, and finished reading an article from the latest hair magazine and saw her phone begin to vibrate.

"Hello?" Chrysta said not recognizing the number.

"May I speak to Chrysta?" A male voice boomed on the other end.

"This is Chrysta."

"Hi, Chrysta, this is Jesse. How are you?"

"I'm fine." Chrysta said automatically. "I'm sorry who is this, again?"

"Jesse . . . . from yesterday with the tow truck."

"Oh, oh yeah. Okay. What's up?" Chrysta said.

"My boy Reggie towed the car to your Grandma's mechanic last night."

"Okay, thanks." Chrysta said less than enthused.

"Anyway, I wanted to see if you were okay, and if you needed a ride anywhere."

*Silence.*

Chrysta sighed. "Look Jesse, I appreciate what you did." Chrysta prepared.

"Hold-up, wait a minute . . . I see where this is headed . . . . I'm a man you just met, and it seems like I'm being overly nice to you for no apparent reason. The truth is I don't want anything. My mother thinks a lot of you. Besides, you ain't the only one havin' hard times. I just wanted to help out cause I saw there was something I *could* do. But the offer is still on the table . . . you need a ride somewhere, my number is on your Caller I.D."

"Well . . . Ummm." Not quite knowing how to respond. "Cool. Thanks. And tell Mrs. Smith I will see her at her hair appointment Thursday."

A few seconds later, Chrysta was off the phone. She walked over to her dresser mirror. Staring at her reflection, she reminisced about her 'bouts with men for the past few months.

"Regardless of how attracted to Jesse I am; Regardless of how much he pretends to care for me without even knowing me, I know what the deal is and I'm officially done with men for a while."

She combed her shoulder length hair into a smooth ponytail, placed a Satin scarf on it and walked down the hall to check on Morgan one more time before she went to sleep.

In the parking lot, Jesse sees a slim looking dude spraying the tires on his Impala.

"You Ced ain't ya?'" Jesse inquired.

"Who wants to know?" He shoots back.

Jesse gets out his car, walks slowly up to Ced and gives him a stern warning.

"Yo' my man. You know what you did, and you know that I know what you did.

"Whatchu talkin' 'bout playa?'

"Chick up there in 310. Her and her grandmama. You set that up."

"Mane." Ced states nervously.

"Yeah you did."

Ced reaches for his keys and heads to his trunk.

"Yo Ced, check this out." Jessie goes over to a stool nearby, brings it back over, slings it up about three feet in the air, strikes it with his fist and the stool is obliterated into countless pieces.

Ced is floored by the demonstration and stops dead in his tracks.

"That's your warning, bruh.' Stay far, far away from her." Jesse warned.

Jesse got in his car and drove off.

Later in the night, Chrysta awakened from her sleep in a near-panic state. She got up to walk around the house to make sure that all the doors were locked. The door that the robbers had kicked in had been replaced by maintenance the day of the robbery. But Chrysta was still shaken and had developed the routine of waking every morning at one or two, double checking everything before she felt comfortable going back to sleep. She checked the kitchen to make sure the pistol was in the same place, just in case she needed it again and tiptoed back to her room to go to sleep. She lay there, closed her eyes and fell asleep again.

# CHAPTER THIRTEEN

*A real friend is one who walks in when the rest of the world walks out.*

~ Walter Winchell. Journalist

## Sunday dinner

"Mama Jane! Your meals just keep getting better and better. There is absolutely no way in the world I can resist your smothered pork chops, macaroni and cheese and turnip greens, let alone anything else on this table." Kimberly said.

"I know that's right," Janice said as she bounced Joshua on her lap.

Chrysta had started encouraging them to take walks at the high school a few miles away after dinner. So Janice and Kimberly went and put Travis, Traniece, and Joshua down for a nap while the boys played video games and the girls played dress up in Morgan's room.

"Chrysta, girl, I've already lost 14 pounds from your lil' Sunday walks after dinner. And I've been walking more during the week. Anymore and I'm going to disappear." Kimberly said.

"Well you look great. Size 6?" Chrysta asked.

"Size 4, now but I *was* a size 12." Kimberly said.

"Imma 4 too." Chrysta said. "Now I have a good excuse to raid your couture closet."

They both laughed. "My *couture* clothes came from consignment, so if you're cool with that, raid on." She said to Chrysta. "Janice I KNOW you've lost a ton of weight."

"Yeah, I think that all that walking with y'all and breastfeeding helped to get me back down too. I'm a 6, now." Janice answered.

"I thought so." Kimberly said.

"My clients have picked up," Chrysta began as they continued to walk "And I'm getting my money up, so I'm thinking about getting an apartment next month." Chrysta beamed.

"That's great news Chrysta!" Kimberly shouted.

"Girl, I know you have wanted this and have been working on it for a long time!" Kimberly said.

"Yes, I have, and we've all been working hard in school. Will you be leaving right behind me, Janice?" Chrysta asked as she and Kimberly leaned over and looked at Janice.

"I'm happy for you but I gotta be honest, as much as I want to leave General Oaks, it's bittersweet for me." Janice said as she started to get winded from walking fast. "Coming here saved my life. I was able to start over here. The rent is cheap. And the roaches and the sirens will never overshadow that for me." Janice said.

"Yeah, I grew up here so I feel ya' but I can't wait to leave." Chrysta said.

Afterward, they went back to Mama Jane's, and Janice and Kimberly got their children together and went home to get ready for another week of work and school.

The next day, Kimberly saw something that caught her attention on the way home from work.

Two doors down from her bungalow, she saw furniture being set on the street. She pulled up into the driveway; got out of her car and walked up to the gentleman that was laying the furniture out on the street.

"Excuse me," she said.

"Yeah." The broad shouldered man with the tool belt said to Kimberly as he began rushing in the opposite direction.

"Hi, I just wanted to ask about the house here. What's going on?" she said walking back toward the front door trying to keep up with him.

"You gon' have to move lady, I'm trying to hurry up and get this done." He said, coming back out with a large glass mirror.

"I understand. I just wanted to know what happened to the owners." Kimberly said.

"The people that lived here lost the house. I work for the bank, and the bank told us to come over and clean it out for resale."

"Do you know how much it's going for?" She asked.

"Lady, do I look like the banker? I just clean 'em out and move on to the next one." The man said.

Kimberly smiled. "Thanks so much for your help. Oh by the way, what bank is it?"

"Third Federal." He snapped and ushered her along her way as he finished up.

She couldn't help but smile on the way back to her car. She had a year's worth of savings in the bank for a project and at the right price; this could be her first renovation.

*   *   *

Chrysta took Tariq, Tre', Porcha and Morgan to the mall on her babysitting night.

"I wanna go to the toy store Mommy." Morgan said as they passed by.

"Sure." She said. "Is that okay with you guys?" She asked Porcha and Tariq.

Chrysta looked down at a puzzle-faced Tariq and said, "I promise we'll stop at a 'guy' store next okay, Tariq and Tre'?" She said slightly laughing.

As she was walking into the store behind the kids, she thought that she saw someone familiar out of the corner of her eye. She had. It was Raymond. He was walking toward the play area with three ice cream cones. He gave one to a little girl who had bounced out of the jungle gym, ran toward him and sat down beside him.

Chrysta wondered what she would say to him if she ran into him again. She concentrated on it for days after he left her and her daughter outside in the rain. Chrysta took a closer look and could see that the child favored him. Raymond licked the second cone and held the third as he looked around at the different stores surrounding the play area. Then he caught a glimpse of Chrysta. She was four stores away, but he recognized her right away. All of a sudden a woman with five large shopping bags came and sat down beside him. The giddy well-dressed woman planted a kiss on him as if they were madly in love, and she had not seen him in weeks. Raymond nonchalantly kissed her back and handed her the ice cream cone. He cast a piercing look back at Chrysta as she watched the woman with the huge engagement ring, and platinum wedding band walk over to watch the little girl on the slide. Chrysta returned his stare, noting the wide wedding band on Raymond's finger matching that of the woman that just joined him. Chrysta told the kids that she would be right back and that she was two steps away. She struck a devilish grin and marched out of the store over to where Raymond and the woman were sitting. She approached the woman and reached into her pocket.

"Ma'am, I'm sorry but I just could not help but notice," she said leaning down to whisper to Raymond's wife as if she were just a stranger passing "what a beautiful head of hair you have." Raymond turned around in shock.

"Oh, thank you!"

"Do you have someone who does your hair on a regular basis?"

"Actually no. I just go to whoever's at the mall salon."

"Hummmm . . . . Well, here let me give you one of my cards. You've got a beautiful head of hair. I'd enjoy working with you. I'm trying to build up my clientele. Who does your daughter's hair?" She said as she gestured toward the little girl playing in the jungle gym.

Raymond looked on in disbelief.

"Oh I just braid it at home, but she's getting to that age where she is getting particular about styles."

"Oh, I know all about that. I have a daughter too. I'm Chrysta Perry by the way. And you . . ."

"Sloan Meadows." She replied.

"Your hair is just so beautiful and full and healthy. I can't help it, do you mind if I feel it?" Chrysta inquired.

"Uh. No. Not at all." The woman replied.

Raymond kept staring.

Chrysta bent sideways directly in front of Raymond's face revealing a hot pink thong to shake the woman's hand. Raymond sat in utter disillusionment.

"Oh, how rude of me, hello" she said to Raymond. "Is this your husband?" Chrysta asked Sloan.

"Yes. Honey, this is Chrysta Perry." She excitedly told her husband.

Raymond, still in a state of shock, could barely say hello, so he gestured it with a raised hand. A thin line of sweat was forming above his bare top lip.

"It was so nice meeting you Mrs. Meadows; I don't want to interrupt your family fun any longer she said eyeing Raymond on the sly. I really hope we can do business soon."

"Likewise. I look forward to it."

Chrysta snickered as she walked off and positioned herself to throw one more dart. She took out her cell phone and shot Raymond a quick text. Quickly she stationed herself behind a mall sign and peered his way. Sending the text through, she saw him feel his waist, peel his smart phone out and view the message. He read it, looked up and his bright skin turned as white as a sheet of paper.

"I'M BACK. Checkmate, ho!"

She was giddy as she trotted off.

All of the children were sleeping on Chrysta's floor on blankets after returning from the mall and eating dinner. Kimberly and Janice were still in class. Chrysta lay in the bed reading and her cell phone began to vibrate on her nightstand.

"Hello?"

"Hello, Chrysta?"

Yes?

"It's Jesse."

"Oh, hi Jesse. What's up? You need a haircut?" She asked.

"Funny, it's been a year and I still haven't made it into your favorites?" He said.

"Now who's being funny?" she said.

He had called a few times before, but Chrysta had held to her promise of no men 'til she was in a better position in her own life.

"Actually, I was just thinking about you, Chrysta, and wanted to call and ask if . . ."

Boom, boom, boom!

"Chrysta what was that?" Jesse said interrupting himself hearing something like fireworks in her background.

"Hold on . . ." Chrysta ran to her window to see where the noise was coming from.

She could hear men yelling profanities at each other. It sounded like two or three men at the least, and they were coming from the next building.

"Jesse, I need to go so I can figure out what is going on." Chrysta said in a rushed and nervous tone.

"I'm coming over!" Jesse said.

She had told him about the robbery that happened right before they met last year one night when he called and they had talked on the phone. That was his immediate first thought. "I just want to make sure everything's okay."

"Let me try to figure out what's happening, bye." Chrysta said, not hearing his last statement.

With that, they hung up and Chrysta dialed Janice and conferenced Kimberly in. They had told her that class was canceled that night, but she said to let the kids stay over so they could study so she figured they were home.

"Did you guys hear that?" Chrysta asked.

"Yes! What is going on?" Janice said in a panic.

"I hear an ambulance," Kimberly said.

"Hold on, Imma call Shaleathia. She lives in 105, closest to the main street and can probably see whatever is going on," Chrysta nervously said running her words together. "I'll call y'all back."

"Girl, they shootin'!" Shaleathia said immediately when she saw Chrysta's name on her screen.

While Chrysta was on the phone with Shaleathia, she heard a knock at the door.

"Was that a knock at your door?" Shaleathia asked. "Girl you bet not get that. Fools' is crazy tonight. Hold on, I got a beep." She said.

Chrysta nervously walked to the apartment door and peeped through the peephole.

"Chrysta it's me, you ahight?" the voice called out.

"*Jesse?*" she said quietly to herself.

"Jesse what are you doing here?" She said opening the door.

"I was at my Mamma's house, and I didn't hear the shots over there but heard it through your phone when we were talking. I figured they were closer to your side and I wanted to make sure you, Ms. Jane and Morgan were okay.

"Mama Jane?" she called out. "Come on in Jesse."

"Huh?" Mama Jane asked Chrysta as she walked into the living room and saw Jesse.

"Are you okay?" Jesse and Chrysta asked her at the same time. "Yes I am, and I checked on the churren and they're fine. No stray bullets through the windows or nothing."

Shaleathia finally got back on the phone and Chrysta sat silently for about three minutes.

In the meantime, Mama Jane introduced herself.

"Young man, my name is Ms. Jane Perry, but most everybody calls me Mama Jane. You are?"

"Hello. My name is Jesse Smith and my grandmother is your neighbor. I was just visiting her. Oh you're Polly Mae Smith's grandbaby. Okay. Lawd, time flies. I remember when you were a speckle in your Mama's eye. Sit on down in here. What brings you over?"

"Actually, I came to check on Chrysta, you and Morgan after I heard those shots."

Chrysta hung up from talking to Shaleathia. She called Janice and conferenced Kimberly, while turning to Jesse and Mama Jane and said,

"Okay, y'all. You know Jordan, the crack dealer . . . the one with the corn-rows? He got murdered outside. Shaleathia said police found him lying face down".

"OOOOHH! Breaking news on Channel 4 ya'll!" Kimberly yelled into the phone.

## Channel 4 News

The reporter, a clean cut gentleman, appeared on the screen. He began his report:

> "There has been a homicide, including three fatalities that we know of in the General Oaks Housing Community, and the community has been locked down. Law enforcement is asking all General Oaks residents to stay inside their homes. The task force is performing an area-wide man-hunt. They are looking for a black male . . . light complexion, black eyes, black hair, with a scar on his left cheek. He is approximately 6'2" and was last seen wearing a dark blue jacket or sweatshirt and dark jeans."

The next morning, everyone was tired. Chrysta had fallen asleep with her head on Jesse's chest as he slept on the couch. Mama Jane was in her room with Joshua, Travis and Traniece who were still peacefully asleep, she had been up for an hour and had checked on Morgan, Porcha, Tre' and

Tariq in their rooms. After four hours, the police finally issued a statement that the armed men were most likely out of the area and the community was taken out of lock down status. They did include in their report that one of the victims only 13, was a junior high student and a member of the boys and girls club.

# CHAPTER FOURTEEN

*The secret to productive goal setting is in establishing clearly defined goals, writing them down and then focusing on them several times a day with words, pictures and emotions as if we've already achieved them.*

~ Denis Waitley

Twenty *missed* visitations, twenty-six *uncollected* child support checks and four parent teacher meetings alone, Janice found herself at the park with Jaurice at his request. It was in the mid-seventies and the sun was shining and he told her that he wanted to talk to her then spend the rest of the weekend with the children.

Janice watched Tariq and Porcha run toward the swings.

"Thank you for not aborting my baby." Jaurice said to Janice as he sought eye contact from her.

"Thank you?" Janice asked nonchalantly looking at him briefly then back at the children playing.

"Yes. I've wanted to tell you that for months now. I hit bottom when you left. That's why I got drunk that night I heard you were having Joshua. That house wasn't the same. I moved; I ho'd around; I changed jobs." Janice rolled her eyes and shook her head. "Life was not the same, and I realized that the life I was chasing was right at home all the time. No one could replace you. You're my life. You're my future. And I want to thank you for raising my sons and daughter. You've always been a good mother."

"Jaurice." Janice interrupted, barely able to keep her lunch down.

"Janice let me finish. I realize that hitting on you was wrong, doing it in front of the kids was even worse. I know I am not my father and I ask you to forgive me. You are such a good mother—such a good woman." Jaurice said.

Janice smiled slightly and then looked up into his face. "Are you finished?"

Jaurice nodded. "Jaurice, I know all of those things. I don't see a future for us. Please, have my babies at the coffee house at 6pm tomorrow night so I can take them home." She walked away toward the swings, kissed each of the children, Tariq with his ball and glove, Porcha on the swings, Joshua in his father's arms and walked away, not looking back.

*  *  *

Kimberly had done her homework on the potential renovation down the street from her bungalow, and found that the bank that owned the house just wanted to get rid of it and was going to sell it for $30,000. She gathered her paperwork together, sat on the bar stool at her tiny kitchen island in her bungalow after the children were asleep and called DeMarco.

"DeMarco? Hey big bro." She said smiling.

"Hey lil' sis. What's going on?"

"I need to ask you something about a potential investment."

"Okay, shoot."

"Well, you know that I have always been interested in architecture, and building and renovating. Since I have been back in school, I have been saving to buy a second house, and renovate it to see if it would be something that I would like to do on a consistent basis.

"Uh-huh." DeMarco said, letting her know that she had his full attention.

"I have a 750 credit score so I have already been approved for the capital for the foreclosure two doors down to start my renovation on, but I don't want to work alone on the project. I would like for you to partner with me on this." Kimberly said as she started to pace around the island.

"Kimberly, I believe in your drive, and that you will be successful at anything you put your hands on, but you've never renovated a house before so I have a few questions." DeMarco said. "Do you think that this would be time to do this, with the kids so young AND you being back in school? Do you know enough about houses in general?"

"I've done a lot of research and you're forgetting one important thing; the fact that I do own my own home and have been keeping it up by myself for the last two years." She said confidently. "You're right, I have thought about my schedule, and that is one of the reasons I wanna partner with you. It would help to have two extra eyes and ears that I trust to oversee the project."

"So what would be the real role that you are asking me to play? I mean the hands on role—you know I'm not a handyman." He chuckled. "And I don't think you'll be doing all this work yourself."

"I'm just asking you to be a silent partner. I know some handymen from my little house projects over time. We could use the same team for renovating this project. I'll set the schedule up and everything else; I just need you to have my back." She said.

*Silence*

"Let me see it first. Snap a picture of the house for me and forward it to my phone. If it looks okay, I'll bring a $15,000 check over tomorrow." DeMarco said.

*   *   *

Janice arrived at the coffee shop an hour early, and grabbed a seat to work on some homework. She was patting her feet to the sounds of *Kyoto Jazz Massive* playing in the background while getting her books out of her bag, when she noticed that Chrysta was there, sitting at a table in the back, alone. Janice grabbed her purse and went to say hello.

"Hey Lady, whatchu doin here?" She said giving Chrysta a broad grin.

"Hey yourself! Chrysta said returning her smile. "I actually don't know why I'm here, girl. Sit down real quick," she said looking around. "Shameka just called me out of the blue yesterday toward the end of my shift, and asked if I could meet her here."

"Girl, you 'bout to get a raise. I know you are. All those new clients you've been bringing in, you've been handling yours." Janice told her.

"You think so?" Chrysta said, her eyes widening.

"Yeah, I do—oh, I see her coming this way. I'll talk to you later." Janice quickly got up and headed back to her table.

"Hey Janice. Long time no see." Shameka stopped and said to Janice as she nearly arrived at her table.

"Yeah, I'm going natural. Chrysta and I have talked about it." Janice said smiling at Shameka

"Well it looks great, but you'll still need a little bit of maintenance and trims."

"I know, that's what we've been talking about." Janice said.

They both laughed.

"If I know Chrysta, you two will be talking 'til you're back in that chair."

"Exactly," Janice laughed and said as she looked over toward Chrysta.

They said their goodbyes, and Janice sat down to do her work and waited for Jaurice to bring the kids.

The next day Kimberly took the day off to put together her loan application for the bank to start her renovation.

"Hey DeMarco . . ." she said opening up the door for her brother.

"Hey." He said smiling while walking through the door. "You got something to eat?"

"Boy you always hungry and never gain no weight." She said hitting him jokingly on the back of the head.

"And *you* always got food. I know you got some banana bread up in here! You always do."

"Yes I do."

"Can I get some milk with that?"

"Yes, you may."

"Cool." He said.

So," he said reaching into his inner pocket in his jacket. "Here it is." He handed her a sealed white envelope and removed his jacket to get ready to eat.

"I appreciate this, Marco."

"Just go get my money, baby girl. I want to see you happy and doing what you love but make no mistake, I'm motivated by money and want to see a profit too."

They both laughed.

"I see you been putting the paperwork together. Tell me all about it." He said pointing his fork at the paperwork lying on the island.

Kimberly sat down with him at the kitchen island eating warm banana bread, and cold milk as they went over the loan application and worked together on a budget for the renovation.

Janice stumbled in to work exhausted and cranky. Joshua was teething and everyone in the house was suffering.

"Janice, these came for you early this morning."

"What did?" she said, not looking back at her co-worker, who had walked up behind her as she took off her coat and hung it up.

The co-worker said nothing. Janice turned around and saw a bouquet of 24 white roses.

"Oh, how pretty!" Janice gasped.

"I thought so too." She said.

Janice took the card out and began reading it silently.

"Everybody has seen them and commented on how gorgeous they are. You are one lucky woman." The co-worker said.

"If only you knew," she said under her breath as she excused herself to the bathroom with them.

Beyonce's *Check On It* blared from Chrysta's speakers as she conferenced Janice in, after getting Kimberly on the line later that afternoon.

"I got news y'all!" She said, adjusting the volume.

"Okay, let's hear it girl, I went on break to take this call." Janice said.

"A'ight, Shameka wants to open a new shop, and since I have just as many clients as she does, she wants me to run it!"

"Congrats girl! What else is she offering?" Kimberly asked putting Traniece in the play-yard in the living room.

"Offering?"

"Yeah. Surely she's offering you a grip of money and a cut of the profits."

"Hummm . . ." Chrysta said turning the CD player completely off this time.

"I'm happy for you but that is a lot of responsibility, and I'm not telling you what to do or nothing but if it was me, I'd be pushing for some sort of ownership on this. I mean I've been in there, seen you in action, and you have enough clients to open up a shop of your own."

"I've never thought of it that way." Chrysta said.

Janice congratulated her and told her she had to go back in to work. Kimberly stayed on the phone with her, and talked about the deal for twenty more minutes.

\*     \*     \*

Janice and Chrysta, I want you to come to church with me." Kimberly said as she picked the twins up from Mama Jane's the next afternoon. "I went last Sunday and had a good time."

"Don't they call that "Club Neezer" down there?" Chrysta said as she chuckled. "Mama Jane said she can't get no *true* religion down there."

"Right, my Aunt GG said the same thing." Janice said.

"Well they may not, but that's a different generation, we have different needs. Besides y'all, I don't think it would hurt just to visit, would it?"

"I don't guess so. I'm in." Chrysta said.

Kimberly turned closer to Janice and softly and said, "Janice, you're not going anywhere anyway. You know while you were in the hospital having Joshua, I met your Aunt GG and she said that you used to love to sing and play the piano in church. Come on, you'll enjoy it." Kimberly puckered her lip out and pleaded with her.

"Alright, I guess it wouldn't hurt." Janice said, "But I need to let you ladies know that we got to get up early. When I got to church, I never embarrass myself by walking in late."

# CHAPTER FIFTEEN

*Most great people have achieved their greatest success just one step beyond their greatest failure.*

~ Napoleon Hill

Kimberly's class was canceled that night, and she decided to go over to the library and get ahead on some of the work that was due in a couple of weeks. As she rushed through the doors and turned the corner in the lobby, she bumped right into Cole Harlan.

"Hey, Kimberly!" Cole looked ecstatic to see Kimberly.

"Hey Cole." Kimberly said. She looked at her watch and continued to walk.

"I haven't seen you since you turned me down for that date you know." He displayed a wide grin as he stepped closer to her.

"Right." She said.

"Soooo . . . which one of our classes will the lovely Miss Mayes be studying for tonight?"

"Actually, I'm reading Chaucer and working on functions tonight, so it's going to take a lot of concentration."

"You didn't think I would let the fact that you've turned me down once, deter me from asking you out again, did you?

"Of course not." She shot back and walked forward with him following.

"Well here goes . . . Kimberly, I'd like to take you to a movie and get a little dinner."

Kimberly turned and looked at Cole and said nothing.

"Still not trying to go out with a brother are you?" Cole said smiling and shaking his head. "You're missing out Miss Mayes." He said.

"Am I now?" Kimberly said as she smiled and walked away.

"I'm breaking you down Miss Mayes, I can tell. You 'ain gotta respond . . . I already know."

"'Ain gotta?' Who did you take for English?" She turned and asked.

"Maybe *you* could tutor me." Cole said getting louder as she continued walking away from him.

"Too busy." She whispered and threw her hand up waving bye to him. *He's fine but gotta focus,* she thought.

Kimberly got a table at the library, placed her coat and purse on the table and began to set her books, pencils and notes up for a two-hour study session.

## Later

As Kimberly showers, Malik enters behind her totally nude. The familiar dark, heavy chest hair lined his chest all the way down to his stomach.

Kimberly melted as he touched her from behind, and she felt his warm legs against her backside.

"You remember that huge house on three acres we always used to talk about?"

"I remember." She replied as she drifted further into his embrace.

"I think I changed my mind." Malik stated. "It could be any size as long as you are there in it with me."

"You sure?" She asked.

"Positive."

Kimberly turned to kiss him. No one was there. Devastated, she began to cry uncontrollably; wondering *why am I being tortured*?

Three days later, Kimberly, Chrysta and Janice walked into the wide vestibule of Ebenezer International Church, stepping on several crunchy leaves that had sneaked in on the heels and boots of several other worshippers preceding them. Kimberly made eye contact with one of the ushers. She pointed upstairs letting Kimberly know that the main level was at capacity. Once up there, one of the five ushers showed the three of them to their seats.

"Jaurice said he was actually taking the kids to church today." Janice leaned over and whispered to Kimberly and Chrysta once seated.

"Really? That's good, right?" Kimberly asked.

"What? Is he going to do Porcha's hair? Does he know how to comb it?" Chrysta interjected.

"I guess it's good Kim. Nawl, I braided it last night after he called." She answered both women.

"Good." Chrysta said. I don't want anybody touching my god-daughter's hair after all that work we've put into it over the past year." Chrysta shot a smile at Janice.

They both nodded in agreement. Chrysta had spent the evenings, when Janice was in class, braiding and caring for Porcha's half-inch brittle hair. She had grown it out to shoulder length, almost half the length of Morgan's and she was picky about who touched it, sometimes even Porcha's own mother.

"Those checks still coming?" Kimberly asked.

Janice shook her head, "He's had three jobs in the last year, so he's missed a few."

Kimberly shook her head and the music began. It was loud and electrifying. They began to see people jumping up and down, waving their hands in the air in praise.

Janice stared at a family sitting in front of them. A woman with a little girl that was about two years old was sitting beside her on the left, and a man was sitting closely on her right, holding a baby boy only a few weeks old in his arms. The baby looked as if he were beginning to whimper, and the woman pulled a pacifier out of a bag on the floor and handed it to the man. Janice broke out of her daze when a voice called out through the speakers that the church announcements were beginning.

*Welcome to Ebenezer International Church, here are your announcements.*

A man's voiceover sounded over the picture of a microphone and several instruments along with the words "Gospel Reign Contest" growing on the huge screen said: *Do you have a gift of singing, leading a worship service, playing an instrument? Well here is your chance to show off your abilities to your friends and family but especially to the Lord. Sign up for the 2006 Gospel*

*Reign Contest today. It will be held here at Ebenezer International Church on Saturday, November 4*[th]*. There will be a booth for sign-ups in the atrium, beside the bookstore, immediately after service.*

Kimberly cut her eyes over to Janice to try to get a sense of her interest, but saw nothing.

They sat through service. Kimberly noticed that Janice and Chrysta seemed to enjoy themselves.

I thought that was nice to see." Janice said after the dismissal, when the singing began.

"What's that?" Kimberly asked.

"Men sitting with their wives in church, and holding and taking care of the babies." Janice said.

Chrysta burst into laughter. "Girl please, I know half these guys. It's really not what it looks like." She said.

"Dude in front of us, for example owns the hottest strip club in the city, *Club Pop It*. I know y'all heard of that. I can't believe he has enough energy to make it up in church with his "still tryin' to get that ring" girlfriend, and I ain't talking about a lack of energy from running 'the business side' of his business, by the way."

"Anyways . . . This was fun, we'll have to do it again sometime but I gotta run. Thanks for the invite Kim."

They all hugged. And from there, Chrysta disappeared into the sea of people filling the vestibule to head for her car.

"Well, did you like it?" Kimberly asked Janice as they walked slowly through the crowd.

"That music." Janice almost stopped. "You were right. I *really* enjoyed the music. The church I grew up in was small, and we did not have many instruments or people who could play. But the full band and the sound system; the music just seemed to fill your body like it was air."

"Wow, that's awesome that you were able to connect like that. What did you think about the announcement for the church's singing contest? I think it's right up your alley, girl!" Kimberly got right to the point.

"Yeah, I thought about that after the announcement. That's why you *had* to have us come this Sunday. I dunno Kimberly. It's just been so long ago . . . almost like it was another life or something. You'd probably have a better chance of getting me to go to *Club Pop It* than enter that contest, and you know that ain't happening."

"Well, hopefully you'll change your mind and when you do, just remember, auditions are in like two weeks. I think they've been announcing it for 4 or 5 weeks already." Kimberly said.

They walked past the contest sign-up booth, and the crowd of people waiting to be transported to their cars by the church buses to the overflow parking, to their own cars on the hill above the church.

*     *     *

An hour after service, Chrysta sat in the coffee shop waiting for a 15—minute late Shameka to discuss salon business, that she asked her to meet with her to discuss.

"Hey lady, I'm glad you could make it, and I'm sorry we have to keep meeting on Sunday afternoons like this, but you know this is the only day that our clients aren't knocking at our doors. We are so blessed right now to have so much business." Shameka said as she sat down with Chrysta.

"Yes we are." Chrysta smiled.

"So, I wanted to talk to you about the details of the new shop I'm starting. I know you're excited and said that you had some questions about what was in it for you, and businesswoman to businesswoman, I respect that." Shameka said.

"Good." Chrysta said. "So let's hear what you've got."

"I want to be straightforward with you. I can't offer you any ownership in my company Chrysta." Shameka said. "You're a good stylist but you graduated with my niece Shaleathia what, two years ago?"

"It was three actually." Chrysta corrected.

"You're young, you haven't been doing this long is what I am saying, and I'm not saying I won't ever have a place for you as a partner when I am ready to actually take on a partner, but give yourself that time to become more seasoned."

"I see." Chrysta said. "So how long are we talking?

"A couple of years, maybe, but it may take only a few years. A decision like that cannot be made lightly, and I have been working on this almost my whole life." Shameka said taking a sip of her coffee.

"I understand that. I have been working on hair my whole life too."

There was an awkward silence between the two of them until Shameka said, "Ummm, I took the liberty of bringing over a contract for you to look over." Shameka said. "It doesn't included what you are asking for but Chrysta, I am offering you a name as a top stylist in a salon that has been around for a long time and at a healthy cut at that. I wish I had had an opportunity like this at your age."

Shameka slid the contract across the table at her.

"Shameka, I appreciate your offer." Chrysta looked down at the contract but did not touch it. "I don't think that you realize though that even though you have been around for fifteen years, you ran the salon out of a two bedroom house on Ewing Drive for the whole fifteen years. And within the first six months that I was there, you had to look to move to a commercial space when my clients started basically bursting the seams of the building."

Chrysta slid Shameka a sheet of paper across the table.

"Here is a list of those clients, by the way. Shameka, I love working with you and I have learned a lot, but we both know that I could have *my own* salon right now. I'm studying business at school and will have a formal degree in it eventually. I've almost single-handedly grown your business. Why not give me the recognition I deserve in part ownership?"

"I won't do it." Shameka said as she looked over the list in anger. "I won't become a partner with a twenty-one year old shampoo tech."

"I'm sorry that you see me that way. I see something much *much* bigger." Chrysta said standing.

"Well, I'm sorry we couldn't reach some sort of agreement that was mutually beneficial to both of us today. I will continue to pay my booth fees as usual, and see my clients at the Ewing Drive location and I do want to wish you good luck with the other location. I'll see you at work tomorrow."

Shemeka said nothing, just stared at Chrysta.

Chrysta grabbed her bag and left, leaving both her list of clients and Shameka's contract on the table.

＊　　＊　　＊

The next Saturday, Janice had fed all of the children, and had their bags and toys lined up at the door. It was 4pm and Chrysta and Kimberly would be showing up in about 15 minutes.

Janice, coughing and sniffling, went to the cabinet to see if she had some of the kids cough syrup left from last winter. She heard Joshua (who was supposed to be sleeping) stirring around and headed back in the living room to check on him. On Joshua's face, crawled a large cockroach. It tickled his face as it crawled from his forehead to his cheek in a seemingly drunken, fast and frenzy confusion. Joshua whimpered scratching at his face and Janice ran quickly screaming, grabbed it off of Joshua and took it to its death.

She pulled a crying Joshua out of his playpen and held him.

Five minutes later, when Janice opened the door for Kimberly to pick Tre', and the twins up, Janice looked at her and said,

"Kimberly, do you have a program from Sunday? I need the number to that Gospel Reign Contest."

# CHAPTER SIXTEEN

*Whatever course you decide upon, there is always someone to tell you that you are wrong. There are always difficulties arising which tempt you to believe that your critics are right. To map out a course of action and follow it to an end requires . . . . courage.*

~ Ralph Waldo Emerson

Janice went to Ebenezer International Church the next day but did not tell Kimberly or Chrysta. She thought she would run into Kimberly there but did not see her. She brought Tariq, Porcha and Joshua with her. She told Karen she was still able to have a great worship experience on the phone that afternoon, before Karen had to catch a plane to Wisconsin for a conference for work.

After that conversation and several sneezes, she went to her room and lay across the bed with the phone in her hand. Porcha and Tariq were playing loudly and running around the house, but Joshua was asleep and that was all the permission she needed to try and get a nap in.

"One week 'til the contest and I'm coming down with a monster cold." Janice said to Kimberly after she called Kimberly.

"You need to call Mama Jane and . . . uh . . . uh . . . let her tell you . . . uh . . . what you need to get to take care of that." Kimberly said, clearly distracted.

"Now I'm getting nervous. I can't sing if I'm sick." Janice said. She heard Kimberly hammering on something loudly in the background. "What are you doing?"

"I'm knocking a wall out . . . well, starting to before the team comes in tomorrow to finish it. Listen, Janice, everything is going to be fine. Call

Mama Jane. She's helped me with tons of remedies over the past year and a half for the twins *and* Tre and I. Call her. Listen, I gotta go but I'll call you a little bit later, okay girl?" Kimberly said.

"Okay." Janice looked out of the window and the sun was starting to set on another chilly day in General Oaks.

*   *   *

"I know I can do this Mama Jane. Run my own salon, make it the hottest salon in Nashville, I know I can do this."

"Chile' it takes money for somethin' like that. A lotta money. And you don't wanna start it, then halfway through find out that you can't pay yourself or nobody working for you. You know what I taught you." She told Chrysta.

"I know, Mama Jane."

"I know what? Let me hear it?" Mama Jane demanded.

"Right now?" Chrysta asked.

"Yes right now. Let me hear it." She said.

Chrysta sighed and said,

"When a task is once begun
never leave it 'til it's done,
big or little great or small,
do it well or not at all."

"You just remember that little girl and you'll be just fine." Mama Jane smiled.

*Ring . . . ring . . .*

*Ring . . . ring . . .*

"Who is it calling, Chrysta?" Mama Jane asked.

Chrysta looked at the phone next to her arm on the kitchen table and said, "It's Janice."

"Alright, lemme have it."

"Okay, Mama Jane. Imma go do Morgan's hair."

"Alright Precious. You remember what I said."

"I will." Chrysta walked out of the kitchen toward the back of the apartment.

"Hi, baby." Mama Jane said answering Janice's call.

Kimberly looked down and read the checklist Chrysta had written earlier and smiled.

"The Salon Sunday campaign looks like a winner, girl! Five women can book appointments every Sunday morning from 5am 'til 10am to look Salon Fresh before church service." Kimberly read. "That's brilliant! I told you that you could do it. You'll have the city in your grip before you know it. Everyone will want to come to your salon."

"Thanks." Chrysta laughed as she looked around. "That's encouraging."

"Oh and I saw that look on your face when you walked in. It's dull and dreary now, but wait 'til I finish. Let me show you."

"I'm going with an open concept. This is going to be the living room, dining room and kitchen. It's going to all be in one big open space and make the whole entire house look larger and more modern."

"Well, you sound like you know what you're doing and I like the way you keep your house so even though I can't see it, I know it'll be cool." Chrysta told Kimberly.

"Thanks, that's encouraging!" Kimberly said. They both laughed.

Well, girl I gotta go so I can finish here and go get the kids. They are spending some time with Malik's parents. But remember what I told you; don't leave Shameka's 'til you absolutely have to . . . you still need a steady paycheck and time to develop your plan and make it iron clad." Kimberly said as she walked Chrysta to the door.

"I will, and that is a smart idea." Chrysta said.

"I'm glad you came by." Kimberly said.

"I am too, I'll see you later." Chrysta yelled back as she turned the ignition in her car.

An hour later, Janice was sitting in Mama Jane's kitchen sipping on a hot toddy while Joshua was still sleeping and Porcha and Tariq sat watching a cartoon. The aroma of the liquor, spices and sugar rose in the air filled the kitchen.

"This oughta' get you better in a day or so. Then you can get back to practicing your song for the contest. I know you gon' do well!" Mama Jane told Janice as she walked back to her apartment.

"Thank you so much! I may not be going to work tomorrow . . . just so you know, if I don't get by here with Joshua." Janice said.

"Okay baby, just you let me know. Now, if you need to rest though, you can bring him on ova." Mama Jane said.

"Okay, Mama Jane." Janice said.

"Just call me if you need anything at all." Mama Jane said.

"Alright, night."

One week later, Ebenezer International Church was decorated with long shiny curtains on the stage. There were blue, red and multicolored lights everywhere. People with earphones and clip-boards walked with a quickened pace all around the backstage area.

Janice was sixth and there were three acts following her. Janice's name was called and she started walking towards the stage. She wore a black skirt, white cotton blouse and flat black shoes that she got from a thrift store since she was in between sizes. One of the ushers nearby offered his hand to help her up. She took it and walked onto the stage. She saw Kimberly, Karen, Chrysta, Aunt GG, and Mama Jane all sitting in the audience . . . all there to support her. All the kids were there and Mama Jane was holding Joshua, who was being unusually calm.

She sat down at the piano. She began to sing and play her rendition *Something Inside So Strong,* and all the memories of her childhood flooded her mind. She closed her eyes and saw herself cleaning the country Baptist church with her 70-year-old grandmother. They brought the communion trays that they had washed at home using their own well water pulled from the ground. Janice hurried her sweeping job, so that she could get to the piano and practice on it. She did not know one technical note, only the notes that came from her head and heart. She began to play with more passion. She came to the bridge and rested her voice a moment, and that memory dissolved into her adulthood, her marriage, her decision to drop out of school. She saw herself giving birth to her kids. She began to sing and play with even more passion. She passionately took her voice, and the melody of the piano through the pain and struggles that she felt over the past 5 years.

The house bandleader noticed her in the moment, and silenced the band so that the only sound that filled the giant auditorium was Janice's passionate voice and the melody of her piano; she played 'til the tears rolled down her face. Then the bandleader gently led each instrument back in one by one.

Forty-five seconds later, Janice rested her fingers on the last six keys and stood to face the audience that was already standing for her. She saw

Aunt GG's face first. Tears. Tears were being wiped from Kimberly and Chrysta's faces.

Kimberly mumbled, "I didn't know you could sing and play like *that!*" so that Janice could read her lips.

There she stood with two other finalists at the end of the show. The first place winner was on track to a recording contract with a major recording house, a manager, and twenty-five thousand dollars in cash plus local endorsements. For the second and third place winners, there were gift certificates.

"And the winner of the first annual Gospel Reign Contest of Nashville is . . . . she moved us and took us places in her music we didn't expect to go tonight, Janice Rivers". Janice stood there on stage in shock. The second and third place winners grabbed her and hugged her, but she was numb. She looked into the cheering crowd and saw Aunt GG jumping up and down, with Chrysta and Mama Jane dropping a single tear with Joshua still in her hands. Kimberly was pointing to her, and talking to Tariq and Porcha like she was explaining what had just happened. Then it soaked in like a sponge that had been dropped in a bucket of water. "Oh my God, I must have won!" She thought to herself. Janice began to cry. She was still numb and didn't know how to react. She had never won anything before.

Everyone from Janice's clique rushed the stage: kids and all. Afterwards, she met her new manager and a couple of music execs that were thrilled to make her acquaintance.

"Janice Rivers, everyone" the host said lastly, prompting the crowd to cheer. That was the last thing that she heard before she felt Kimberly and Karen raising her hands in the air toward the crowd like an Olympic gymnast after she'd won gold. Then they took her hand and guided her offstage. Karen holding her hand on one side, and Kimberly on the other. Two women in white dresses motioned for them to follow them to the back of the church.

"Mama! Deddy came. I saw him!" Porcha said almost yelling as she ran backstage to her mother with Chrysta, and Kimberly holding Travis walking behind her.

Chrysta tossed a cynical look over at Kimberly who returned it and they both looked at Janice who seemed to be holding a painted on smile, said, "Oh really? Did you have fun tonight?" she asked pulling away from the subject.

"Yes, ma'am." Porcha said.

"You were good." Tariq said to his mother, almost shy and slightly star struck.

"Oh thank you baby." She bent down to hug him and turned toward Kimberly. "Where is everyone else?"

"Joshua is being fed, and rocked back to sleep by Aunt GG. Mama Jane is holding Traniece, and Morgan and Tre' are sitting in the seats beside them." Kimberly said.

"Oh yeah," Chrysta interjected. "Jaurice came over to us and was like just standing there. I guess he is waiting for you to come out." She said.

"Okay," Janice said, as calm as ever and rose up from hugging Tariq.

The contest staff came into the dressing room where they had all gathered, and went over Janice's contact information one more time, and told her to expect a call from them for several meetings that would go forth in the next few weeks on Monday.

They walked back out into the sanctuary and the church had mostly emptied. Janice walked quickly over to Aunt GG and Mama Jane, and gave them hugs and kisses on the cheek. She also hugged Morgan and Tre', and as she did, saw Jaurice walking toward her in her peripheral.

Kimberly cleared her throat and when everyone looked over at her, she tossed a look at Jaurice and Janice and said, "Let's go everybody."

"I ain't gotta leave, hell. He ain't talkin' bout nothin'." Aunt GG said holding Joshua in her arms. "An' this baby heavy as hell, Janice, you been feedin' him pig feet and chitlin's already?" Aunt GG questioned Janice as they were all walking away. Janice shook her head and smiled at her aunt.

"Here, let me take him." Karen said.

Janice looked to her left, and saw men feverishly working on taking equipment off the stage, taking banners down and wrapping up what looked like hundreds of feet of cable. Trying to make the church look like church again for the 7:15 am service.

It was almost midnight, and they were the only people standing in the large three-level sanctuary that were not working.

"I really enjoyed your performance." Jaurice said as he put his hands in his pockets and stood tall in front of Janice.

"Thank you. Thank you for coming, I didn't really expect to see you here."

There was an awkward silence and Jaurice said. "Listen, I um, know it's your weekend but I wanted to see, you know, if you wanted me to take the kids home with me tonight, seeing how you've had a long night and stuff. I thought you might want some rest."

"That's nice of you, but I would really like nothing more than to wake up in the morning and fix my children some breakfast." She said then looked down and around again.

Jaurice stepped closer as if he was trying to kiss her, but Janice stepped back. "Jaurice," she said. "Thanks again for coming." She turned and walked away to catch up with everyone and walked right into Timothy.

"Hey brother-in-law. I thought you were working tonight and couldn't come." Janice said.

You know I ain't gonna miss out on this. I'm proud of you." He gave her a hug as he continued talking to her. "Karen told me that you were in here alone talking to Jaurice, and I thought I would just stick closely by. Come on, they're right outside the door. I'll walk you."

Timothy turned and made eye contact with Jaurice, who had watched Janice walk away and was still standing there.

Janice looked up at Timothy and smiled. He was like the brother she never had.

"Are you thinking what I'm thinking?" He asked.

Yeah," she looked back at Jaurice who was still standing there. "Ain't no future there."

"Girl, you're a mind-reader." Timothy said.

# CHAPTER SEVENTEEN

*I'm a great believer in luck, and I find that the harder I work, the more I have of it.*

~ Thomas Jefferson

Early Sunday morning and five hours after Janice's performance and big win, Kimberly left the kids sleeping in their beds, locked the door, set the alarm and walked two doors down to check on her renovation. After a week, her contractor and his crew had knocked out all of the walls out between the kitchen, living and dining rooms. They scraped all of the tile and linoleum off the floors in preparation for the hardwood laminate she was having installed throughout. She still had to accomplish the plumbing, electrical, installation of cabinets and appliances, and of course the staging. She also had to create some additional curb appeal to the property before the open house, which was six weeks away. *Gonna be a successful flip.* She thought as she looked around.

She walked to the back of the house and opened up her notes section in her phone.

*Note to self* she wrote. Talk to DeMarco about going shopping for the new appliances, counter tops and cabinets for the kitchen, on second thought, cabinets will remain to save money.

She closed her note section on her phone . . . walked around once more and locked the door to go back to her bungalow.

After church, Kimberly called and asked Malik's parents to keep the kids so that she could work on the renovation. She figured if she could pick out and schedule delivery for the furniture for staging early, which would be one less thing they would have to wait on.

"DeMarco, this flip is going so well." She twirled in an animated spin in front of him. "I've decided that my goal would be to flip 100 houses. If I make a minimum of $10000 profit each, I'll net a million dollars."

"Wow, now that's a goal." DeMarco said. "The numbers sound good but the financing, the pace, and how long will it take you to flip a 100 houses?" He said putting his arm around her.

"If I can manage a job, three kids, and a house on my own how much harder can this be? It is simple math and Imma go for it. Are you in?" Kimberly asked.

"Kimberly, I believe I remember saying two or three houses. Now I am glad this one turned out so well, but they can't *all* be like this, you know that right? I just don't want to see you get disappointed. By the way, Mama told me that you have been spending a lot of time shuffling Tre', Traniece and Travis between her and Ms. Perry and Malik's parents. Is this becoming too overwhelming?"

Kimberly turned defensive. "Ya know, for someone chasing *their own* dream right now, you don't seem to be very empathetic to me chasing mine."

"I don't have children though." DeMarco shot back.

Kimberly stared at DeMarco for a moment, and then turned toward the front door to walk out.

"Kim, I'm sorry." He said as he ran out after her. He gently turned her toward him with his right hand on her left shoulder. "I just . . . you know I have issues with Mama not being around for us when we were little. I resented her for it. I don't want the kids to experience that. You are all they have." He said.

"I know that! Don't you think I know that? I was forced into playing Mama and Daddy and nobody ever lets me forget that!" Kimberly cried.

DeMarco grabbed Kimberly, and held her in the living room as she cried aloud.

\*　\*　\*

The next weekend, Chrysta swept Janice's weave up into a ball, smoothing the edges with shaping cream while her hot comb heated.

She looked at the large mirror with a hundred light bulbs around it and quickly inspected how she had pinned her own hair up that afternoon for resemblance. Her first performance since the contest, was for a breast cancer benefit in Brentview. She was nervous but glad to make the extra $800 for the evening.

"So how close are you to getting your salon, Chrysta?"

"Actually, I've done a lot of research, but haven't talked to a realtor or anyone that can actually take action steps and help me make this happen yet."

Janice grabbed Chrysta's hand, interrupting her work on her hair. "If you need anything at all, you let me know."

"Okay." Chrysta said.

"No, I mean it. Promise me you will let me know." Janice insisted.

"I will."

"Good, because you have done so much for me; I want to help you anyway I can."

"I appreciate that, girl. I really do. And hey thanks for calling me to do this gig with you. Anytime you need—"

"Yeah, I wanted to talk to you about that," she said, almost interrupting, "They have lined up four more of these over the next two months, and I wanted to see if you could come out and do my hair again for all of them? I'll give you the same cut and add a little extra if you can throw some makeup on me."

"Absolutely!" Chrysta was overjoyed inside. "How do you want your make-up?"

"Just do want you want. I just want to perform my music." Janice winked at Chrysta and turned back around.

Chrysta finished pinning her hair up for the show that evening. She walked out to take her place at Janice's table and spent the rest of the evening enjoying her performance.

∗    ∗    ∗

The next week, it was all that Kimberly could do to stay awake in her office. Between taking care of Tre, the twins, and being at the property every day for as long as she could stand it (including being there before and after class twice a week), she was exhausted. But she could barely hold in her excitement, as she told anyone who would listen about her experience of taking a dilapidated house and turning it into a modern day showplace.

Yet, Kimberly decided to stop by her mother's house after work for a quick hello and see if they needed anything.

"Hey Ma." Kimberly said.

When Genesa opened the door, Kimberly walked in slowly looking back and forth between her and her boyfriend Roger shaking her head.

"What is wrong with you, Kimberly?" Genesa said walking back over to sit in her matching recliner next to Roger.

"Mama . . . I could smell the reffer as soon as I got out the car." Kimberly said, and then rolled her eyes.

"I tole' ya', yo' behind need to call somebody fo' you come over here. You onno what might be going on over here . . . grown up in here." Genesa said as she pried the joint from Roger's two fingers.

"Keep messing wit me Roger, ain it'll be a roach fore it get back to you!" Genesa yelled.

Before Kimberly knew it, an argument broke out, she said her quick goodbyes to Roger and her mom and left.

\*  \*  \*

After the weekend engagements, Janice tried to catch up on her sleep during the week but with the children and her job, it was difficult. Even four engagements and two weeks of hardly being at home had exhausted her.

It was 6pm and the kids were just home from school and day care, and Janice found herself dozing off when the phone rang.

"Hello?"

"Hey Jan."

"Hey Karen. What's up with you?"

"Everything is good here. What about up there? How are you and the babies?"

"We're good." Janice answered.

"You sure? Timothy told me about what happened after the show the other week. Sounds like somebody is trying to pursue you."

"Yeah, girl. He is. I'm not trying to hear it, though."

"You sound sleepy and I know it's been a roller coaster these past few weeks so I'll be brief. I hope I'm not overstepping my boundary, but

Timothy and I paid for three sessions with our accountant for you. We actually started using an accountant way before we started making a decent salary, and we're glad we did because I feel like not a penny has been wasted. Anyway, I know that you shared with me some of the checks that are coming your way and I just want you to have the same feeling."

Janice nodded as intently as she could even in her state of exhaustion. "Thanks, sis that was thoughtful of y'all."

"Yeah and if you don't like her, you'll still have an idea of where the money has gone or is going thus far. If you do like her, you can continue with her but you'll definitely need someone on your team with your best interest at heart to help you manage that cash flow." Karen advised.

\*   \*   \*

Chrysta had begun to work on a list of the things that she thought she would need for her new salon, after her initial meeting with Shameka at the coffee house. She had started writing a little bit on the list every day since. She was looking over the list late that night, and as she checked her list, the home phone rang. It was late and Mama Jane was asleep so Chrysta hurried out of her room and around the corner to answer the one on the kitchen wall with the long chord.

"Hello?" Chrysta answered.

"Well, well, well, if it isn't the stylist to the stars." The old creaky voice said on the other end. Chrysta could barely make out that it was a female. She had the voice box of a chain smoker.

"You mean to tell me you done know ya own mamma when she call." She said more as a statement than a question.

"Deidre?" Chrysta asked.

"Ding ding ding ding! That's right puddinpop. Well you *is* smart—and talented I hear. Listen, I need my hair did and I thought you could pass me a couple of dollars too while you were at it. I been hearin' about all these women's heads you been doin'. And here I was thinkin you were still in Junior High. Whew time shole flies!"

"Deidre, you call me at 1am in the morning to ask me for this? Are you serio—?"

"Let me have the phone, Chrysta." Mama Jane came from out of nowhere and took the phone out of Chrysta's hands. "I'll handle this. Go on back to bed." Mama Jane stood there holding the phone with her left hand, her right hand cuffed around the microphone at the bottom.

"You hear what I told you? Gwawn back to bed now." Mama Jane said.

Chrysta focused a cold gaze at the phone until she finally backed up and went to her room. She heard Mama Jane get on the phone, and whisper a reprimand to her mother before she slammed the door.

# CHAPTER EIGHTEEN

*I am not afraid of storms, for I am learning how to sail my ship.*
~ Louisa May Alcott (1832-1888)

"Girl, Joshua's teething and he 'bout to drive me crazy!" Janice said.

"I know how that is. I mean, TJ hasn't been that age for a while now, but I remember it. You're going to have to put an egg above his bedroom door overnight." Karen said.

Janice pulled the phone away from her ear, and looked at it as if her sister were crazy.

"Hello? Are you still there, Janice?" Karen asked.

"Yeah, I'm here." Janice said as she smiled and shook her head.

"You may not believe me, but just watch him settle down after you do that. Just try it Jan, it works. So . . . how is everything going with your music contract? Did you speak to the accountant?" Karen asked.

"It's going good and I did speak to the accountant. The money is rolling. It's sweet. I have some shows coming up out of town, but to be honest, I can't really see myself going out on the road all the time Karen, you know I have kids."

"This is a different world." Karen explained. "You can hire an assistant to help you with them while you are out there. What is important is that you have a unique opportunity to provide for yourself, and your family—possibly for a very long time."

"I know, and I WILL take advantage of it. I just need to figure out a way to do it on my own terms." Janice said.

"I know you will baby Sis. I'm so proud of you. Not only for putting yourself out there and sharing your amazing talent—then winning, but for being brave enough to step out and create a new life for yourself, your children and for being strong enough not to be sucked back into your old lifestyle with Jaurice." Karen said.

"Thank you, sista. That means the world to me." Janice said.

Over the next four weeks, Janice continued singing and playing at the church, shows, and wherever she could with whomever would let her.

After seeing the passion Janice had during that concert, the church's music director asked her to stay and speak with him for a moment that Sunday.

"You know, Janice, you have a unique ability to hear music, write it and arrange it." He said as he leaned on the piano that she was playing after their rehearsal. "I've witnessed that over the past few weeks. Not everyone has that talent. I really want you to work with me on producing the church's first children's album. I was wondering if you would be interested." The music director said.

"I would love the opportunity to do that." Janice remarked.

They talked for another half hour about the project, and the director set a time for a more formal meeting two days after that.

Once she had accepted that position, with money in the bank and her accountant's blessing, she felt confident enough to make her next move. She went to work the next day to put her plan in motion.

She sat at her work station with her 22-year-old co-worker and chatted between calls. The girl over the past couple of months had talked nonstop about her family in Brentview, how she has been to rehab twice, her bulimia, her suicidal thoughts, and shopping addiction. Janice calmly listened to her problems, as she had so many shifts before and said, "I have found that people like me that grew up with the same background, spend the rest of their lives trying to un-complicate life, and kids that grow up in loving stable homes spend the rest of their lives trying to make life complicated. You chew on that for a minute, Sweetie. I'll be back."

Janice walked over to her manager and asked if she could speak with her during her break . . . . to resign.

\* \* \*

Kimberly was on her hands and knees wiping down the baseboards inside her property. It had been an intense few weeks and they were finished. The only thing left to do, was stage it and place the for sale sign in the yard.

Kimberly bought the house for $30,000, sold the house for $79,000. After spending $15,000 on the renovation, she and DeMarco netted $34,000 —which was exactly what she made as an assistant at Broch.

"I've got a gift for you." DeMarco said as he walked around their first finished renovation.

"Where is it?" Kimberly said looked around for a gift bag or box of some kind.

"I got the $7,500 back that I put in and that's enough for me Sis. You worked so hard, I want you to be successful at your next one, so I want to give you my half of the profit."

"What?!" Kimberly nearly screamed.

"I'll sure take my share of the profit on the next one though." He said smiling.

She ran up to him, and gave him a tearful bear hug. *Things are finally falling into place for me.* She thought to herself.

She spent the rest of her evening trying to convince DeMarco to invest in two neighboring duplexes for their next flip. She had already cleared it through their inspector. DeMarco was in.

\*     \*     \*

Janice stepped up to Mr. Duke's duplex. It had been 3 years since she had knocked on that door, but it seemed like a lifetime.

No one answered.

She knocked again.

No one came.

As she turned to get into her car, she heard the door latch snap, then the door swing out on creaking hinges.

Mr. Duke looked exactly the same.

Janice walked back up to the door, and Mr. Duke stared at her. He searched her face. No bruises. No swelling. No discoloration. He hugged her as if he had no intention of letting go, and she hugged him back.

With no words yet spoken, she followed him inside, glanced over at the infamous hanging beads separating the bedroom from the living room and sat down. When they finally spoke, he wanted to know everything that had been going on with her. She caught him up on everything, and thanked him for his care and concern during those hard times in her life. But even as she recounted the contest, her endorsements, and her move to her house, nothing seemed as impressive as the smiling face across from him with no evidence of abuse.

\*     \*     \*

The *Whisper Song* played on her portable radio as she tried to prime the walls of her new salon, following the directions that Kimberly had given her.

Chrysta was now a salon owner of a space in the trendy *Down South* district.

The next day was opening day and the first person to sit in Chrysta's salon station chair after Janice, who did lend a financial hand and was responsible for the opening, was Sloan Meadows.

"My husband is a sleazebag." Sloan said to Chrysta after greeting her and congratulating her on her new place.

"You remember don't you? He was there at the mall with me that day. I'm sorry, but I gotta get this out. I suspected he had some philandering ways, so I hired a private investigator and I got more than what I asked for on him for the past couple of years." Sloan said angrily.

Chrysta nearly lost her breakfast with that statement. "Really, girl?"

"Yeah, he gave me all the information on one chick, and I told him I didn't want to see anymore. I never knew how good it felt to wrap a Gucci belt around a little 20-year-old tramp's neck." *Twenty?* Chrysta thought to herself. *He still likes 'em young.* "I sweated my hair out so bad, I need another relaxer. Can you hook me up?"

Chrysta relaxed. "Wow, sounds like you had one interesting day."

Sloan went on to give Chrysta the details blow by blow while Chrysta calmed herself and prayed. *Those days are behind me,* she whispered to herself.

When Chrysta finished Sloan's hair, she looked her in the eyes and said, "I'm truly sorry for what you have gone through." Chrysta gave her a warm but uneasy embrace as they finished their session.

\*     \*     \*

Janice began getting calls from other labels in the music industry, including country, the genre that her city was famous for, to come and produce songs for them.

She had built a solid portfolio and reputation with the music she had written and produced for the gospel album, and some other studio work with new artists in the city—mostly hip hop.

Janice walked into *Urban Studio 615* in sweatpants, a t-shirt and baseball cap, revealing a long bushy ponytail. There was a room full of men sitting at the mixing board with their cell phones out, playing with them occasionally and popping there heads and necks to the beat.

Janice spoke to them, placed her designer bag on the nearest table, took out her tablet and began to make notes on the tracks they were playing, occasionally asking questions.

It was 5 hours later before she could actually get to the board herself, and adjust the gain, pre-amplifier, pre-faders and equalizers to her liking. Because the kids were with Jaurice this weekend, she had time to stay and get into the sub grouping as well. Otherwise, she would have left hours ago.

Janice was at her wits end with the antics inside some of the studios, but she needed the money. She also needed to make a name for herself in the predominantly male driven industry. So, she took every offer on every song, on every album that she could.

Two days later, she called Kimberly.

"Kimberly, girl can you talk right now?" Janice asked.

"Sure," Kimberly said, placing some of the paperwork for Broch's finance department aside. "Let me close my door."

"Everything ok?" Kimberly asked.

"Yeah girl, things are fine. I just feel like I need to go ahead and get another place, and I was hoping to get your help." She said.

"You know I'd be happy to!" Kimberly replied.

"Here's the thing—I have some things that I would *have* to have in this house." Janice warned.

"Oh yeah? Ok what are they?" Kimberly inquired.

"The studio I go to always have people smokin' weed, girls always hangin' out and dancin' and stuff. It's just buck-wild, over there. I need my own studio."

"Ok. That shouldn't be too hard, as long as you are willing to spend a little bit for it." Kimberly said.

"Oh, I am. I'm passionate about my music, and I need to be able to handle my business each and every time I sit at the board. Oh, and it needs to have a separate entrance in case I invite a serious artist over to record and work. I don't need anybody walking all through my house to get there."

"Ok, got it. What's your budget?" Kimberly asked and pulled out a blank sheet of paper from her desk.

Kimberly and Janice talked about the budget and a few locations around the city that they would have those kinds of specs in a house. Kimberly told her that she would come over after work to discuss it further and went back to crunching numbers in her office.

*   *   *

Very early in the morning, Jaurice was asleep in his mother's house. Suddenly, two sheriff's deputies awake him as he feels the cold steel of one handcuff locking one wrist while folding his other arm around his back and locking the other wrist.

"Hey! What ya'll doing? What I do?" Jaurice complains.

One deputy answers, "Bench warrant for unpaid child support."

The two deputies lead him out of the door, and down the porch into the waiting squad car.

# CHAPTER NINETEEN

*The key to realizing a dream is to focus not on success but significance—and then even the small steps and the little victories along your path will take on greater meaning.*

~ Oprah Winfrey

A few years had passed since Kimberly had flipped her first house. Afterwards, she developed a voracious appetite for deals. She would thumb through the newspapers, real estate magazines and log on to real estate sights every chance she could. Kimberly received a real rush after every real estate flip which she always netted a profit on. This eventually led to more lucrative deals. In her most famous deal to date, she built a business complex that not only housed *Chrysta's House of Style Beauty Salon*, but also an insurance company, a cash advance store, a retail clothing store for women, an attorney's office, a pizza house and a full-time janitorial service. Business was so good, Kimberly had to hire her home girl Chrysta to manage the complex. As Chrysta was now able to hire some of the best young beauticians the city had to offer. It also got Chrysta away from her main past time, man-watching.

Kimberly was everything to Janice and Chrysta. They had not only a healthy respect for her, but adoration; an almost mythical love for a lady who never gave up in spite of. She was beyond question, someone who inspired them to live up to their potential. She remained the person who they could count on no matter what.

In 2013, Kimberly, Janice and Chrysta rang in the New Year together with all of their families, which had not changed much. They had been working hard with their ventures over the past seven years.

Chrysta opened three salons and netted $100,000 her first year. With the addition of her products, spa services, and the only place that catered to Sunday clients, her income continued to double every year.

Kimberly did help Janice get her dream home. Janice had produced her way to the top as one of the highest paid producers in the country. Her assets from royalties on hit songs she had written and produced, placed her well over the million dollar mark years ago.

Kimberly sat in her office and calculated her assets. One million, three hundred thousand, seven hundred thirty five dollars and forty-three cents; a tear fell from her eye.

She had finally just placed her bungalow on the rental market as a three-bedroom apartment on the main level; and a finished two-bedroom, one bathroom basement apartment, 5-7 minutes from two of the nation's top colleges. It turned out to be the perfect place for a group of college students.

The next Saturday afternoon, Kimberly called Janice and Chrysta on the phone.

"Chrysta?"

"Yes."

"Janice?"

Yes.

"Ok, I just wanted to make sure that I had you two on conference."

"You know I hate surprises Miss." Chrysta whined. "This is my absolute busiest day at the salon and I have put the afternoon aside just like you asked."

"Thank you Miss Chrysta." Kimberly said smiling into the speaker phone.

"Yeah, you're welcome," she said jokingly.

"Yes, what is going on Kimberly? I didn't schedule myself to be in the studio today for whatever was so important. You better be telling us you have gotten engaged or something. It betta be huge!" Janice warned.

"Gotta be huge." Chrysta echoed.

"Well, I don't want to make you wait any longer, so I just wanted to call you and let you know that I was on my way. I don't want you to look for my car though; I'm in a black SUV. Chrysta, I should be picking you up in about 10 minutes and Janice, we'll pick you up in about 20. Ok?"

"Wha?" Chrysta remarked. "Miss I budget, I splurge on nothing." Chrysta said.

"I know you have been busy for the last few weeks, but it looks like we DEFINITELY have some catching up to do." Janice said.

"We sure do." Kimberly replied, smiling through the phone.

\*　　\*　　\*

## Brentview

Kimberly picked Janice and Chrysta up and they talked nonstop about everything. Finally she rounded the shiny new wheels into a subdivision no more than 20 minutes from General Oaks. Pulling into the driveway, Janice and Chrysta took their sunglasses off and peered through the semi-tinted windows of the large truck.

"Oh my goodness, Kimberly!" Janice and Chrysta said almost simultaneously. Kimberly had opened the garage door to a 2 story, 5 bedrooms, 4 ½ bath 4300 square foot house.

"Girl, this is what you are about to buy?" Chrysta asked almost screaming.

"I already bought it . . . for cash." Kimberly said nonchalantly.

"What!" Janice and Chrysta said in unison.

"Wow, Kimberly. That's amazing."

"Well, let me show y'all the inside."

"Exactly!" Janice said almost running to the door.

## The Tour

"Ladies . . . the grand tour." Kimberly said proudly as she placed the key in the door and turned it.

"This is the foyer, Ladies." Kimberly said as she entered and sheepishly stepped to the side.

Chrysta and Janice were amazed at how beautifully laid out it was. The entrance had a marble floor that had a unique asymmetrical design with soft golden walls, and a ceiling that soared into the space of the second floor.

"To your left is the study and to your right, the formal dining room."

"So Kimberly, when did you close on it?" Janice asked.

Well, it was a foreclosure. I put in an offer a few months ago and they accepted it, but those usually take a while to close. Then I had to renovate it, of course, so a lot of what you see, I got a chance to personally design and do the work. We just moved in a few days ago."

"I love that Kimberly." Janice said in awe of her story.

As they walked further into the house it exploded with space.

"Look Janice," Chrysta said. "I can stand in one spot and see everything."

They laughed.

"Right now you are in the great room." It was an open floor plan that connected to a bar area, with four bar stools facing the kitchen. Turning in a semi-circle, the ladies saw a staircase that sat almost squarely in the middle of the house. You could see the entire staircase, hallway upstairs and the entry to 5 or 6 rooms including one that was very noisy.

"Here, let me show you the master suite first. It's on the main level so that I don't have to hear a lot of the noise that you're actually hearing right now." She laughed.

The walls were a textured cream that led up to trey ceilings. The bed, which was a king, with four large posts and romantic sheer fabric decorating the space between, may have even seemed small in comparison. In front of the footboard, was an upholstered chest for storage but cushioned on top for sitting. The cherry oak armoire in the corner led their eyes to a sitting area beside the two bay windows. Chrysta peeked outside the window and saw an enclosed rock patio with a fireplace, and enough room for three living room sets. The patio furniture surrounded the fireplace, but there was also ample space for the enormous stainless steel grill complete with burners.

"You have a kitchen outside, Kimberly." Chrysta said. "I could fit my downtown condo in your master suite."

"First of all you can't, and second of all, you could afford three of these." Kimberly told her.

Chrysta giggled and they moved on.

The ladies took a quick look into the massive walk-in-closet with a sitting area inside and marble and stone bathroom with glass showers.

"Is that a TV in the mirror!?" Chrysta yelled.

They laughed as Kimberly went on about how every time she went into her bathroom to brush her teeth in the morning, she's greeted with the sports channel, and she knows that Tre' has been in there taking his showers.

The ladies take a peek into the garage, laundry room, gourmet kitchen and two bathrooms and headed upstairs.

"What a view." Janice said. Girl, between walking up the stairs and going across the cat-walk, I can see every room downstairs. This is amazing!"

Tre', Traniece and Travis all had large rooms with walk in closets, and were equipped with computers, desks and bookshelves.

As they were checking out the upstairs rooms, the noise got louder. "Girl . . . Unh-unh!!!!" Janice said as they toured the theater room where the kids were.

The last stop upstairs was the office on the second floor, that Kimberly had wanted with a view overlooking the back yard.

"This is a long, long, *long* way from General Oak's girl! I am so happy for you!!! Not too bad for a mom from the ghetto! You need to let us throw you a house warming."

"You know I accept." Kimberly said looking out of the corner of her eye at Janice and Chrysta leading the way across the cat's crawl.

As they walked downstairs, Chrysta and Janice still talking turned around to see Kimberly's eyes welling with tears.

They immediately walked back up a couple of steps, and hugged her as they sat down together in the middle of the staircase.

Janice rubbed her back and said, "I know that you miss him."

"I do!" Kimberly said. "I do but I am just absolutely overwhelmed that God could take someone like me, a mess, and turn them into a woman that could do what I have been able to do for Tre', Traniece, and Travis. I'm just so thankful right now. And who knew that I would find my best friends at the lowest point of my life?"

They all hugged, with tears in their eyes.

"I appreciate you guys so much! I would have never gotten here without you. You are truly my sisters." Kimberly ended.

Chrysta and Janice chimed in with hugs and nods.

"You know, the most important thing about all of this is," Kimberly said, "if we were to lose our money tomorrow, we would gain it right back again. We have the principles in place, and the formula that made it happen in the beginning. Most of my million is tied up in investments, retirement and my children's college fund. But you know what . . . . I have a million-dollar mentality. That is a blessing in itself."

She, Janice and Chrysta sat down on the deck, of her exclusive neighborhood in Brentview overlooking the rolling hills. They talked about the sound of General Oak's rumbling train that came through every evening, and again at 2am every morning shaking their houses and how peaceful it now was in comparison.

# CHAPTER TWENTY

*You are not here merely to make a living. You are here in order*
*to enable the world to live more amply, with greater vision, with*
*a finer spirit of hope and achievement. You are here to enrich the*
*world, and you impoverish yourself if you forget the errand.*

~ Woodrow Wilson

Six months later, Kimberly walked out of the doctor's office alone, lightheaded, and in a daze.

All of her symptoms had fit. True, she did not fit the profile of other women in her shoes, but the abdominal pain and pressure, loss of appetite and indigestion that would not go away were tell-tell signs. Her doctor, the man that delivered all her children, encouraged her after Malik's death and had become a family friend, was genuine with the schedule of outlined treatment options. But he sat on the other side of the desk in his office with tears in his eyes.

Her whole world was different now. The hospital hall seemed to never end as she walked back to the garage. People were walking toward, around, and besides her going to their various places. Nurses were toting carriers with vials in them to collect blood samples, masked doctors were making their way to the opposite wing of the large hospital, and visitors were coming in to report on patients' progress to family and friends. However, Kimberly felt as if she were in her own world. She heard nothing except the clicking of her heels making contact with the hard, shiny concrete surface.

Kimberly did not even remember how she made it home. The entire afternoon was a blur. She remembered asking Janice to pick Tre', Travis, and

Traniece up from school and calling the contractor working on her latest house that she would not be coming by that afternoon.

Three hours later, it was 2:41 pm and Kimberly lay in a fetal position in the huge empty house staring at the ceiling. She turned over and rolled her petite frame off the high post bed, letting her polished toes sink into the plush neutral carpet. She walked into the bathroom, tied her silky shoulder length hair into a bun, pinned it to her head and stared at herself in the mirror. Just one gray hair . . . and that's all I may get, she thought to herself. Her eyes began to well with tears. Thinking of her children, and how young they were, it just seemed so unfair to her for this to happen to them again. It's just so unreal. She sat on the cold, stone bathroom floor and allowed herself to cry a river of tears.

With her head pulsing from a crying-induced headache, she pulled herself off the floor and walked through the large gourmet kitchen into her office. She sat down in her black leather chair at the computer, and looked around at the beautifully decorated space while it was booting up. Placing her hands on the cherry oak desk, she glanced at a picture of Malik in one frame and a picture of Travis, Traniece and Tre' in another one. Finishing, the search site prompted her to type her command into the field. Kimberly placed her perfectly manicured nails on the white keyboard and typed the letters 'ov' in the box: The search revealed several results: Overstock, ovulation, overhauling and ovarian cancer. Hesitantly, she clicked the fourth choice.

# CHAPTER TWENTY-ONE

*Join in the work of remaking this nation the only way it's been done in America for two-hundred and twenty-one years—block by block, brick by brick, calloused hand by calloused hand.*
~ President of the United States of America,
President Barak Obama.

## Well Done

Kimberly Mayes lay there dying on her bed. It had been four months, and Janice, Chrysta, Kimberly's children, her parents, brother and loved ones were all gathered around. Janice was devastated, and Chrysta is almost inconsolable as she views her friend lying ravaged on the bed. They try, to no avail, to control themselves in front of her family, but they are too stricken with disbelief as they had grown very close to Kimberly in their time together. Weak with parched lips, she can see Malik smiling at her telling her she did good raising the kids, and that he's missed her so much and how he can't wait to see her again. Her body is weary, but her spirit is quite giddy. He beckons her to come on and come quick. The life she's leaving behind is grand, but her job and mission have been completed. Her purpose fulfilled. All the while Malik has been a constant in her subconscious, and her own mortality has now reached a zenith.

She looks into the distance and reminisces about her wedding day. "Kimberly, will you take Malik to be your lawfully wedded husband?"

Kimberly then remembers her first bike, her third grade teacher, her daddy carrying her on his shoulders on the beach, eating jellybeans at the movies, her high school prom, the first time she met Malik, having her children, living in General Oaks and studying for a class she couldn't remember the name of . . .

Kimberly's mother grips her hand real tight and asks her if she feels any pain.

"I do." says Kimberly to Malik.

Kimberly now sees on the horizon a glimpse of what real wealth is, and the warmth of home all over again.

She took one last breathe and shut her eyes.

# THE END

# ABOUT THE AUTHOR

Ukela (pronounced U-Kee'-Lah) A. Moore is a paralegal, author, humanitarian, mother and wife. Ukela is committed to women's health advocacy, financial literacy and family life. She is married to her soul-mate, Terry Moore and they have four wonderful children, KeShawn, Jade, Kenneth and Shawn Nathaniel. She resides in Nashville with her family.

# ABOUT THE CO-AUTHOR

George has authored stage and screenplays including the play High School Skinny and Strange Relationship (coming to the stage, Spring of 2013). A graduate of Tennessee State University, he's married to the lovely Sherri and they have two beautiful daughters, Sydney and Kayla. He resides in Nashville with his family.

# MILLIONAIRE GHETTO MOMS

1) Millionaire—a person whose wealth amounts to a million or more in some unit of currency, as dollars; any very rich person.
2) Ghetto—a section of a city, esp. a thickly populated slum area, inhabited predominantly by members of an ethnic or other minority group, often as a result of social or economic restrictions, pressures, or hardships; any mode of living, working, etc., that results from stereotyping or biased treatment: *job ghettos for women; ghettos for the elderly.*
3) Mom/mother: a. a female person whose egg unites with a sperm, resulting in the conception of a child. b. A woman who raises a child. c. Used as a title for a woman respected for her wisdom and age.
3) Hustling—a to proceed or work rapidly or energetically. b. To be aggressive, esp. in business or other financial dealings.

Proverbs 31: 7-8

"8. Speak up for those who cannot speak for themselves, for the rights of all who are destitute.
9. Speak up and judge fairly; defend the rights of the poor and needy.

Sources:

**All Definitions were provided by Dictionary.com (American Heritage Dictionary)
**The Bible